# THEIR SECRET WORLD

"Deirdre."

She heard Clive's footfalls on the marble floor, now closer, now farther away. He spoke her name again. She was tempted to answer, but resolutely she turned her back to him.

"Deirdre," he whispered, pleading with her. Without warning, he grabbed both her hands and held them tight.

Her breath caught. She looked up at him, at his shadowed face, at his hair glistening from the mist, at his dark eyes. Her hand pulled away from his, and she reached up to touch his face. He leaned closer . . .

"No," she whispered, shaking her head as her heart pounded wildly. "No, Clive, no."

She felt his hands slide behind her back, enclosing her, gathering her into his embrace, drawing her to him even as she tried to push him away. Her gaze met his and she gasped when she saw the fire in his brown eyes, the passion.

In an instant, she was in his arms. His mouth came to hers. She closed her eyes as his lips brushed hers as lightly as a whisper, leaving only to return to touch again and again. She kissed him in return, surrendering herself to him for a long moment. And in that moment he became her world, a secret closed world of their own, the two of them alone in it, together.

# A Most Unsuitable Bride

## Olivia Sumner

**ZEBRA BOOKS**
**KENSINGTON PUBLISHING CORP.**

ZEBRA BOOKS are published by

Kensington Publishing Corp.
475 Park Avenue South
New York, NY 10016

Zebra and the Z logo are trademarks of Kensington Publishing Corp.

First Printing: June, 1993
Printed in the United States of America

# Chapter One

Deirdre looked down on the city as from a great height. Below her the river Thames flowed silently, serenely to the sea; to her right she recognized the ancient Tower of London and the magnificent dome of St. Paul's; ahead of her she saw the spires of the city's many churches thrusting into the clear sky.

The rich scent of roses permeated the air.

She drew nearer, swooping lower, as a bird might, passing over the boats plying the river, looking down on the imposing Houses of Parliament with the summer-green of St. James's Park a short distance beyond, the silence absolute, and everywhere the sweet scent of roses. Now Mayfair lay spread out below her with its ordered squares and stately houses and, as she came closer still, she knew that this magnificent red brick house with the slate roof and the proliferation of chimneys must be her destination.

Fashionably garbed ladies and gentlemen of the ton were gathered in the garden, the June sky above them a soft blue, while all about them roses bloomed in a profusion of reds and whites. This, Deirdre knew *with an absolute certainty, was not merely a wedding party, but a very special gathering.*

*She noticed a short, unprepossessing man among the guests, a man she had never seen before who, though garbed in the height of unfashion, seemed to be the center of considerable attention.*

*As she watched in rapt fascination, the bridegroom appeared, Clive Chadbourne — how could she fail to recognize him? — dark-haired, dark-eyed, handsome, a scar on his left temple. How strange, she thought, since Clive had no such scar when last she saw him.*

*Clive bowed to the unprepossessing gentleman. The man's lips moved, but Deirdre could hear nothing of what either said. The two turned as the bride approached on the arm of Mr. Roger Darrington, Deirdre's father. The bride, her face and hair concealed by a white veil, wore a flowing white gown beaded with pearls. In her arms she carried a bouquet of fragrant pink roses.*

*Clive strode to his bride, murmured a few soundless words in her ear, and then scooped her into his arms and carried her up the stone steps to the terrace. The bride reached up to raise her veil, intending, Deirdre was certain, to kiss her beloved. Deirdre felt the pounding of her heart as she waited for the identity of the bride to be revealed. It must be, it had to be, surely it could be no other than herself . . .*

Deirdre opened her eyes to sunlight suffusing her bedchamber, warning her that she had overslept. She sat up with the memory of her dream vivid in her mind. How real the wedding had been! Or had this been more than a dream . . . was it a foreseeing, a vision of the future, of her future?

As she hurriedly dressed, the certainty grew in her mind that she, Deirdre Darrington, had been the bride in her dream. Though she had never seen the red brick mansion in Mayfair before, and though her family had never been even on the outermost fringes of the Regent's court, in her dream her father *had* escorted the bride and the groom *had* been Clive Chadbourne.

Clive. Her pulses raced as she pictured him in her mind's eye. He was so handsome, so dashing; she loved him more than she could say, she had always loved him. Not with a selfish love, she assured herself, since she desired nothing for herself, she only wanted him to be happy. Deirdre frowned as she recalled the scar she had glimpsed on his forehead, wincing as she imagined the wound he must have suffered to sustain such a scar. Perhaps she had been mistaken, she told herself, perhaps there had been no scar after all.

"You must take the good with the bad and the bad with the good," her grandmother, whose given name was also Deirdre, had often chided her.

Should she tell Grandmama about her dream? Deirdre wondered. No, this would be her secret, a secret to be locked away in her heart, ready to be taken out and savored as often as she pleased. Besides, telling Grandmama of the dream would only serve to discomfit her. Deirdre wanted nothing more than to protect the now elderly woman who had raised her following the death of her mother.

"Dreams are messages from the devil," her grandmother had often said, "as my own mother had occasion to warn me more than once. At first I refused to believe her, much to my regret."

Yet her dream, Deirdre told herself, had been no missive from the devil—quite the opposite. Her fondest hopes would be realized and her impossible wish would become a reality if she, Deirdre Darrington, was really destined to be the bride of the Honorable Clive Chadbourne. There was little doubt in her mind that the promise of the dream would be fulfilled; it mattered not at all that she had last seen Clive more than twelve months ago; she had wished for this for so long, so devoutly, and with such unwavering intensity that her vision must be true.

"Clive Chadbourne is like the brother you never had," her grandmother had said years before.

And Clive had, she was forced to admit, always treated her as a brother might treat a favorite sister. Though she was six years younger than Clive, he had encouraged her to go with him on his rambles over the countryside when he came down from London to stay for the summer at nearby Chadbourne House, had even shown her the hidden entrance to the glen and the path to the knoll overlooking the secluded pool beneath the waterfall that became their special place, their secret place. He had taught her to ride and, risking the displeasure of her grandmother, to shoot.

"Disgraceful!" her grandmother had said, when Deirdre told her. A moment later, however, her grandmother was smiling indulgently, for who could fail to offer forgiveness to the charming Clive Chadbourne? Even Roger Darrington, her father, admitted to having a grudging admiration for her grandmother's sometime neighbor, praising Clive for being proud without becoming arrogant, for being an idealist while never becoming a prig.

Reluctantly setting aside her thoughts of Clive, Deirdre hastened down the stairs while the long-case clock in the hall chimed nine times.

"Here you are, and the day is half gone," Deirdre imagined her grandmother saying as soon as she joined her in the breakfast room. Her grandmother invariably rose well before seven; breakfasts at the customary hour of ten in the morning were not for her.

But her grandmother was not in the breakfast room, since she had finished eating, Agnes told her, more than an hour before. "And then the boy comes with the letter," the maid added.

"The letter?" Deirdre paused with her cup of tea halfway to her lips.

Agnes glanced right and left before leaning forward and lowering her voice. "From your father in London, I expect," she said.

Deirdre caught her breath, frowning in dismay as she recalled her dream. The arrival of her father's unexpected letter—he wrote faithfully once a fortnight and his last letter had arrived less than a week before; this letter must be thought of as unexpected—on the heels of her dream of a wedding could hardly be a coincidence. His letter must bring startling news, perhaps ominous news, and what could be more startling or ominous than the announcement of the impending marriage of the Honorable Clive Chadbourne?

Pushing away her plate, even though the fact that it still contained a goodly portion of her breakfast ham

9

gave her a twinge of guilt ("Waste not, want not," was her grandmother's oft-repeated admonition), she left the breakfast room in search of the older woman.

Opening the door to the library, she found her grandmother sitting at her desk and, seeing how frail the older woman looked, Deirdre's heart went out to her. Her grandmother was writing in the family Bible, which she must have carried from the marble-topped table in the center of the room; the recently arrived letter, she noticed, lay on the desk beside the open book. Deirdre hesitated, puzzled and now exceedingly ill-at-ease, since she knew that only the most momentous family events were recorded in the Bible: births, christenings, deaths, and, yes, most certainly, marriages.

"Grandmama?" she called tentatively from the doorway.

Her grandmother started in confusion at the sound of Deirdre's voice—her hearing had been failing this last year—before looking around her. Seeing her granddaughter in the doorway, she rose and went to her. Leading Deirdre to a rolled-end couch near the window, the elderly woman drew her down beside her, all the while keeping Deirdre's hand in hers.

"Has someone died?" Deirdre asked. She had no aunts and but one uncle, her father's brother, who had emigrated to the Colonies, to Canada. "Is that the news from Father?"

Her grandmother shook her head. "His letter brings joyful news," she said, "not sad. Your father's letter brings word of a wedding, not a death." Yet there was a hint of uncertainty in her voice.

Deirdre's hand flew to her mouth as a sudden frisson of fear shot along her spine; she bit her lip as her fear was followed by an engulfing emptiness when she realized the implication of her grandmother's words. Clive Chadbourne was married! Her hopes, raised so high by her dream but a short while before, were about to be dashed forever by this wretched news from her father.

But wait, Deirdre told herself, her grandmother would have no reason to record the marriage of Clive Chadbourne in the family Bible. Had she once again been guilty of leaping to a conclusion based on the scantiest of knowledge? Thoroughly addled, she blurted, "I dreamed of a wedding, of Clive's wedding."

"Tell me about your dream," her grandmother said — as if, Deirdre thought, she wished to postpone, if only for a few minutes, the time when she would have to share her news from London.

"It was so very, very real." Deirdre hesitated, then described the dream to her grandmother without, however, revealing that she had believed the bride to be none other than herself.

When she finished, her grandmother shook her head with a sadness born of experience. "A man or woman who could actually see into the future," she said at last, "would be a man or woman cursed. Remember this well, Deirdre: no one can foresee; we may glimpse a fragment of the future as through a glass darkly, but what we see there, or think we see there, is so distorted by our hopes and fears it invariably leads us into error. Our futures are found in what we do, not in what we dream."

"Yet I believe in my dream," Deirdre insisted.

"How can you possibly explain the fact that on the same day I dreamed of a wedding, we receive a letter from father informing us of one?" She hesitated before asking the dreaded question. "Was it Clive? Is Clive married?"

"No, not Clive."

Thank God, Deirdre told herself. But if not Clive . . . "Then who?" she asked.

Her grandmother hesitated before saying, "It was your father."

"My father?" Deirdre, though relieved beyond measure that the groom was someone other than Clive Chadbourne, was at the same time taken aback by the news. She stared at her grandmother, all agape. "My father has remarried? After all these years? And at his age?"

"To me, after surviving seventy-five winters, a man of fifty seems the merest stripling." Her grandmother tightened her grip on Deirdre's hand. "Yes, your father has remarried in what was, he writes, a very simple and a very private ceremony." Glancing at the letter resting on the table, she added, "His wife, your new stepmother, was a widow, a Mrs. Sibyl Langdon, now Mrs. Sibyl Darrington, of course. I do believe your father has mentioned her in several of his other letters. And, from the chitchat I hear across the whist table, the captivating widow Langdon was an exceedingly good catch."

"He should have written to me," Deirdre said, as she tried to overcome her hurt. The news had put her decidedly out of humor. Was he hesitant to tell me beforehand, she wondered, fearing my disapproval? Or was he merely thoughtless?

12

"Your father assures me," her grandmother said, "that he will write to you forthwith, but he wanted me to tell you his good news."

Did her father really believe she would consider the news good? Deirdre wondered. If so, how little he understood her feelings. Yet how could he be expected to really know her? She had lived here in East Surrey on the edge of Ashdown Forest with her grandmother, her mother's mother, for almost fifteen years, ever since her mother's death following a short, fever-plagued illness. To Deirdre, her father had always been a distant, godlike figure who spent most of his time in London, a man who generously gave her all she could possibly need, with the notable exception of his love.

"Your father has more news." Her grandmother rose, retrieved the letter from the desk, and handed it to Deirdre. "Here, you should read what he has to say."

Deirdre scanned the first page, punctuated with her father's customary overabundance of incomplete sentences followed by dashes, then turned the sheet over and gasped. "It seems I now have two stepsisters as well as a stepmother." She peered at the paper as she struggled to decipher her father's crabbed handwriting. " 'Phoebe,' " she read aloud, " 'an exquisite miss one year older than Deirdre—blonde with eyes as blue as her mother's. Alcida—seventeen—so very timid— suffers the misfortune of having been scarred by the pox when she was twelve.' "

"How nice for you now to have two sisters," her grandmother said.

Deirdre slowly shook her head as tears stung her

13

eyes. Did her grandmother actually believe she desired sisters? She wanted nothing more than she already had, she needed no one except her grandmother . . . and, of course, her father.

She read a few more lines. "No," she said vehemently, looking up from the letter, "I will not leave here to journey to London next month to live with this new family of mine. And in my stepmother's house, no less."

"Reading between the lines," her grandmother said, "I gather the new Mrs. Darrington brings considerably more to her marriage than two young daughters. You must have realized for some time, Deirdre, that your father has never been a wealthy man. And now, with the war . . ." Her voice trailed off.

Deirdre rose, threw the letter to the floor, and stalked to the window. "I refuse to go." With her hands clasped in front of her, she laced and unlaced her fingers. "My place is here with you."

"Deirdre!"

The sharpness of her grandmother's voice—not since she was a child had her grandmother spoken to her in such a manner—made Deirdre catch her breath. She swung around, ran to kneel at the old woman's side, and rested her head in her lap.

"Darling Deirdre." Her grandmother's tone softened as she stroked Deirdre's red hair. "You belong with your father in town, not here in this lonely, out-of-the-way place. Besides, your duty is to obey your father. He only seeks your happiness."

"He wants me bundled off to London because he wishes me married," Deirdre said, her voice muffled by the folds of her grandmother's gown.

"Only an unnatural father would wish his daughter to become a spinster, and you are, after all, eighteen. Oh, Deirdre, you have such a loving heart, but such a hasty one! How much happier you would be if only you could learn to weigh your words before you speak and to consider all the consequences before you act."

Deirdre sighed. She realized her grandmother was right; and yet, knowing her own impetuous nature, she despaired of being able to follow her advice. She vowed to strive to improve.

"I suppose," she conceded, "that living in town will be exciting; after a time, one must become accustomed to it."

Her grandmother hugged her.

"My dream was so real," Deirdre said. "I was absolutely certain I saw Clive with his new bride. Yet father makes no mention of him."

"But he does. You never finished reading what he wrote."

"He does?" Deirdre eagerly reached out and retrieved the letter. Sitting on the carpeted floor, she leaned against her grandmother's chair and read to herself: "Clive Chadbourne will be with you in a few days—he brings surprising and gratifying news—I promised to allow him to tell Deirdre himself—all my fondest hopes are about to be realized."

Deirdre drew in a deep breath, her heart quickening with joy. She closed her eyes, smiling as she once more pictured her vision of the wedding party, once more smelled the sweet scent of the roses. No longer a spectator, she now imagined herself in Clive's arms, imagined herself listening to his whispered pledges of his everlasting love, pictured herself clinging to him as he climbed the stone steps to the terrace with her in his arms. There she would raise her veil and, yes, she would kiss him.

Her impossible dream was about to come true. Nothing could be more delightful.

How could she endure the suspense of waiting until Clive arrived? The only logical reason for his visit to East Sussex was that, having received her father's permission, he intended to ask for her hand in marriage.

"Oh, Grandmama," Deirdre cried, "how wonderfully, wonderfully happy I am!"

## Chapter Two

Clive did not arrive that day nor the next day nor the next. Finally, early in the afternoon of the third day, when Deirdre had all but despaired, his traveling chaise, drawn by four chestnut horses, rumbled up to the front steps of the house. Deirdre, who had spent a considerable amount of time watching the driveway from an upstairs window, ran down the stairs to the entry hall, where she paused in front of the looking glass to try, with indifferent results, to smooth her rebellious red hair before stepping outside onto the small semicircular porch at the top of the front steps.

A footman swung open the carriage door and Clive, in a dark green waistcoat and black trousers, stepped to the ground. He looked exactly as she remembered him, although perhaps even handsomer, half a head taller than herself, his hair black and curling, his eyes dark and intense. Though now in his middle twenties, he retained the exuberance she recalled so well, a vibrant eagerness, as though he found the world a truly delightful place.

A quick, involuntary glance told Deirdre there was no evidence of a scar on his forehead, not that she had really expected to find one there.

Seeing her, Clive smiled and swept off his gray top hat. He trotted up the steps, looked down at her, blinked in surprise, and looked again. "Deirdre," he said, taking her hands in his, "how changed you are, how very much the young lady."

"And what was I before?" she wanted to know.

"A girl, albeit a most delightful one." Leaning down, he kissed her lightly on the forehead, then took one of her hands in his and strode into the house with her at his side. "Grandmama!" he called.

"If Mrs. Deirdre Fenshaw is *your* grandmother," he had told long ago, "I insist she be mine as well."

"She may be in the drawing room," she told him.

He threw open the door and, seeing Mrs. Fenshaw sitting near the fireplace with her embroidery in her lap, he released Deirdre's hand and flung wide his arms in greeting. "Grandmama!" he cried, and the elderly woman rose and he went to her, embracing her.

"You probably think I traveled here to visit with you and Deirdre," Clive said. "Not so, I came for one purpose and one purpose only—to gorge myself on your apricot tarts."

Mrs. Fenshaw frowned. "My tarts?" she asked vaguely. "Did you once tell me you favored my tarts? Yes, I seem to recall that you did."

He hesitated, holding her away from him to look down at her, not certain whether she was teasing him or whether her memory had begun to fail. "Is it possible?" he demanded. "Could you have forgotten my passion for your tarts? The tarts I always praised as the most delicious in all England?"

The old woman put a blue-veined hand to her chin. "I do seem to recall—" she began uncertainly.

"Grandmama is funning you," Deirdre interrupted with a smile. "I happen to know she is, since she baked two batches of apricot tarts this very morning. She made them especially for you, Clive."

While they feasted on the tarts as they took their tea, Clive talked engagingly of the social bustle of London and gave Deirdre letters from her father and her new stepmother, both telling her how eager they were to have her with them in town at the earliest possible moment. As they talked, Deirdre noticed, Clive frequently glanced at her with a perplexed frown on his face, glanced at her only to look quickly away.

After eating one last tart, he rose and, standing with one hand on the mantel, became serious. "As for myself," he said, "I have gone, as I have heard young men say, to 'list for a soljer.' "

At first Deirdre failed to understand. "Do you mean," she asked, "you intend to enlist in the Army?"

"Not 'intend' to enlist in the Army, I *have* enlisted. Last month I purchased a commission as a captain in the cavalry, and you now see a man on his way to Portsmouth, where I shall board ship to join the Army in Spain."

"Under the command of Lord Wellington?" Deirdre asked. "Have I remembered his new title aright?"

"You have indeed. After being born Mr. Arthur Wesley, he was sent to a post in India, where he became Mr. Arthur Wellesley. Only this past winter he was made the Marquis of Wellington by order of the Prince Regent. Wellington's summer campaign on the Peninsula begins soon, and I intend to be there as a captain in the Eleventh Hussars."

Deirdre's thoughts were all awhirl. She was startled by this unexpected news, alarmed for Clive's well-being, especially when she recalled the scar she had seen in her dream, excited because he was obviously elated by his news, and confused as she attempted to reconcile her expectations regarding his visit with this latest announcement. Was this the sum and substance of the momentous news her father had promised? Or was there more to come?

Glancing at her grandmother, she noted that the older woman's face showed but one emotion, an abiding sadness. "How eagerly young men go to war," she said softly.

"This endless war is almost over," Clive said, "with Bony back in his lair in France after being humbled in Russia, with the Prussians and the Austrians threatening him from the east and Wellington advancing from the southwest. This is a time when England expects every man to do his duty," he said, echoing Nelson, "and I intend to do my part as best I can."

"Yet you have no uniform," Deirdre said.

"Ah, but I do, purchased only last week in town

and now stored in my luggage. Lord Wellington strongly believes that his officers should wear their uniforms only while on duty." He picked up his tea-cup and with one hand behind his back raised it. "A toast. To the defeat of Napoleon; to the end of tyranny, wherever it may be found."

Deirdre's grandmother nodded. "To the end of this terrible war," she said.

Deirdre raised her cup, and when she spoke her voice trembled with emotion. "To your safe return, Clive," she murmured.

Later that afternoon, as she had half suspected, Clive suggested she accompany him on a walk into Ashdown Forest. He had changed into what he called his "country squire garb" of frock coat, buckskins, and top boots. As was his custom, though certainly not the fashion of the day, he wore no hat.

They left her grandmother in the garden at the side of the house, snipping off dead rose heads. Gardening was her passion and, during the growing season, she spent as much time as she could among her roses, tulips, sweetpeas, pinks, and other flowers. No matter how tiring, she liked nothing better than to spend a day collecting seeds and making cuttings.

"While living in town this past year," Clive told Deirdre as they left the garden and started up the path to the heath, "I often found myself fondly re-membering our treks into the forest. So, before leaving for Spain, I want to go back and see it all again." He looked at her in a most unsettling way.

"I came here half expecting to find my memory had deceived me, expecting to discover a smaller, diminished world, but then, when I saw you standing at the top of the front steps . . ."

He stopped abruptly, shook his head, and then strode away from her, turning back after a few moments to peremptorily wave his hand. "Come along, Deirdre, follow me," his gesture said.

She stared at him. How strangely Clive was behaving! An apprehensive chill ran along her spine as she wondered whether she had been mistaken after all. Could it be that he had come here to tell her he was on his way to Spain and nothing more?

You must be patient, she counseled herself. Take heed of Grandmama's words of caution; wait until you have all the facts before you speak your mind. "Wait!" she called after him.

Clive stopped and stood, hands clasped behind his back, until she reached his side, and then they started off together at a fast pace. In a silence that she felt grew more awkward with every passing minute—why did he not speak?—they followed a path to the top of a low hill and onto the moors, a rabbit bursting from the heather to race away at the sound of their coming, the rabbit finally disappearing amidst the bracken and gorse.

Coming to a rutted track, they walked along its grassy verge, stepping to one side to watch a heavily laden wagon from the stone quarry rumble past. From afar they heard the "thwack, thwack," of a woodman's ax felling trees, Deirdre knew, for the timber desperately needed to build ships to replace those lost in the war.

By tacit consent, she and Clive were on their way to the glen, their glen, where the brook known as the Miry Ghyll cascaded over a small falls into a shaded pool. He means to say nothing until we arrive at the glen, she told herself. And then—

Still on the dirt track, they turned to the right and saw, fifty feet farther on, an arched stone bridge crossing the brook. Deirdre ran ahead to lean over the wall at the side of the bridge, gazing down at her reflection in the clear water of the Miry Ghyll. From the corner of her eye she saw Clive, who had been striding after her, stop to pluck something from a vine growing up and over the end of the wall.

When he came to her, she turned and he handed her a pink wild rose—he knew she loved roses—but when she lifted the flower to breathe in its faint scent, several of the petals fell off and drifted down onto the dirt of the roadway. Gazing at the forlorn remnant of the rose, at what she took to be an omen of misfortune, Deirdre blinked back stinging, suppressed tears.

"Pray allow me to pick you another," Clive said.

Not quite understanding why, she shook her head, carefully slipping the rose into a pocket of her white muslin gown. Again looking down at the brook in a vain attempt to hide her foolish, unreasonable tears, she said, "I intend to keep your rose, the better to remember this day." The better to remember you, she added to herself.

When he failed to answer, she glanced at him only to find that his attention had been drawn downstream to the far side of the brook. Following his gaze, she gave a start when she saw a short, unprepossessing-looking man seated on a flat rock with a small sketchbook perched on his lap. When the stranger looked up and saw them watching him, he gave a curt nod before returning to his drawing.

They crossed to the far side of the bridge, where they found a pony-drawn gig tethered beside the track. Skirting the gig, they walked along a path until they were standing a short distance behind the stranger, a carelessly dressed man in his thirties, a homely man whose nose was too large for his face, just as his black broad-brimmed hat was a poor match for his loose brown coat and baggy brown trousers.

He glanced at them, his gaze fixing on Deirdre for a long moment, then resumed his drawing only to put down his pencil after a few minutes. He motioned them to approach.

Looking over his shoulder at his notebook, Deirdre saw a pencil sketch of the bridge with herself and Clive standing behind the stone wall, Clive proffering her the rose. Below the drawing was the inscription, "The Bridge over the Miry Ghyll."

Without rising, the artist said, "Joseph Turner of Twickenham."

"The celebrated watercolorist," Clive said.

Although Turner shrugged when he heard the compliment, he appeared happily embarrassed at being recognized.

After Clive introduced himself and Deirdre, Turner said, "On my way from Twickenham to the southern coast for the fishing boats and the sea and the sky. Nature's grandeur." He paused, then said, "As you see here," and turned the page of his sketchbook.

Deirdre saw another drawing of the bridge, but this was a much smaller bridge, the work of man seeming small and insignificant compared to the trees rising on both sides of the bridge and the menacing arc of the clouds filling the sky above.

He turned to a blank page in his sketchbook. "May I?" he asked Deirdre in his abrupt way. She hesitated, not certain what he meant, then realized he wanted to sketch her. "Only a moment," he said.

"Of course," she agreed.

He studied her intently, gave a quick nod, and began to draw, his pencil flying over the paper. "The vivid red hair," he said, almost to himself, "the high cheekbones, yes, I have the line of the chin, the face and form of a goddess, Romney would have been enchanted."

Deirdre blushed at what she considered an excess of compliments. Clive, looking over the artist's shoulder, glanced from the drawing to Deirdre. He blinked. His expression showed—what? Confusion? Perplexity? Indecision?

When Turner finished the sketch, he swiftly printed his initials, "JT," at the bottom, tore the page from his sketchbook, and handed the drawing to Deirdre. "Never been much for portraits of late," he said, favoring Deirdre with a shy smile. "You tempt me to try my hand again."

When he flipped his sketchbook back to his original drawing of the bridge and began penciling in the clouds—a storm might well arrive before nightfall, Deirdre decided—they thanked him and quietly made their way along the path that led downstream away from the bridge.

"Since I made you the gift of the rose," Clive said, "would you consider giving me your portrait in return?"

She smiled, handing him the sketch and watching as he looked from the drawing to her before carefully folding the paper and placing it in his inside pocket.

A walk of some ten minutes brought them to a thick screen of brush. After holding the branches aside for her, Clive followed Deirdre into the cool, shaded darkness of the grove of trees standing guard at the entrance to the glen. When they started down a steep hill along an animal track, she heard the water in the brook far below them murmuring an invitation.

As they neared the bottom of the gorge, the vegetation became lush, almost tropical, Deirdre thought, with leafy vines twining up the trunks of the trees and ferns growing profusely among moss-covered rocks, the ground dappled by the sunlight slanting through the branches overhead.

They left the track and Clive, his hand protectively on her elbow, helped her descend a steep cleft cut into the rocky slope to the broad flat rocks at the foot of the falls. Looking down into the pool, Deirdre saw bugs skittering across the surface while in the shadowed depths a fish darted this way and that before disappearing beneath a rock.

"This must be what the Garden of Eden was like before the fall," Clive said. "If ever I feel the need to refresh myself, to wash away the grime of the city, this is where I would come."

After she and Clive sat side-by-side at the edge of the pool, Deirdre waited expectantly for him to go on, to talk of this, their secret place, to talk of her and their future together. Instead, he began telling her of London, of the war with France, reminiscing about her grandmother, speaking in fits and starts. As he talked on, Clive, his thoughts seemingly elsewhere, picked up small stones and skimmed them across the surface of the water. She had never known him to be so distracted.

At last, during a lengthy lull in their one-sided conversation, he rose and walked away from her to the far edge of the rock shelf. He returned to stand next to her, looking down at her. He started to speak, shook his head, and once more crossed to the edge of the pool.

He folded his arms across his chest as he stared down into the pool. He glanced to one side at the foaming water at the bottom of the falls, he looked up at the sky as though he might have felt a drop of rain strike his face. With an abrupt nod—he must have come to a decision of some sort, Deirdre decided—he swung from the brook and came to stand over her.

Was it possible, she wondered, that Clive was finally about to ask for her hand in marriage? His actions earlier in the day seemed to argue that he was not, but since she had never in her eighteen years received a proposal of marriage, she was uncertain how Clive or any other gentleman might behave when he arrived at such a fateful moment in his life. Did he fear rejection? Or, perhaps, might he secretly fear acceptance?

"Is there something you want to tell me," she asked encouragingly, "even while you fear what my response might be?"

Clive sat at her side and took her hand in his. "I have wonderful news." His gaze fixed on her hand, he bit his lip as though uncertain how to go on.

"I always welcome wonderful news," she told him.

"Deirdre," he said. He stopped, then began again. Once started, his words came tumbling one over the next. "Deirdre," he said, "while in London I spent many hours with your father, he was very kind to me, and through him I became acquainted with Mrs. Sybil Langdon, now your stepmother, and her two daughters, Phoebe and Alcida, and last week, after purchasing my commission as a captain in the Army, I asked Phoebe—a most charming and beautiful young lady—to be my wife, asked her to marry me on my return from Spain, and I had the great good fortune to be accepted."

Deirdre stared at him in horrified incomprehension. Clive meant to marry Phoebe Langdon, her new stepsister? Impossible.

28

"When we were growing up together," Clive told her, "I recall saying that you were like a sister to me. Think on it, Deirdre, soon you will be precisely that, my sister, not in fancy but in fact. Can you possibly imagine anything more wonderful?"

# Chapter Three

Deirdre, accompanied by Agnes, rode to London in her father's new traveling chaise, stopping every ten or twelve miles at a posting house, where the ostler of the inn cried, "Horses on" and two fresh pairs of horses were harnessed to the chaise and ridden by two post boys resplendent in high white beaver hats, blue jackets, red waistcoats, white neckcloths, short white breeches, and shining top boots. The boys rode to the next stop, where they dismounted and came to the Darrington coachman for their fares before riding the tired horses back to their home posting house. After five changes of horses, they left the dirt, clattered onto the cobbles, and entered London.

Before she left the country, her grandmother had said, "When I was your age, Deirdre, I often thought my life was over after some young man or other—how strange it is that I no longer recall their names or even what most of them looked like—after some young man did something to disappoint or hurt me. But, being eighteen, after suffering through a miserable week or two, I seemed to recover sufficiently to start anew."

Did her grandmother suspect how she felt about Clive, Deirdre wondered, and how devastated she had felt at his announcement that he intended to marry Phoebe Langdon when he returned from Spain? Ever since she could remember, her grandmother had surprised her by being able, or so it seemed to Deirdre, to read her very thoughts. Grandmama was mistaken, though, if she expected a quick recovery, for Deirdre knew with a despondent certainty that she would never be the same again.

Very shortly she would face the ordeal of meeting her stepmother and her two stepsisters, but even more distressing, she would have to live as a member of the same household as Clive's "charming and beautiful Phoebe" until he arrived back in England to claim his bride.

Deirdre vowed to show no ill-will toward her new sister; all she desired, she reminded herself, was Clive's safe return from the war against Napoleon, followed by a life of happiness. Perhaps, in time, if she tried with all her heart, she might even become fond of Phoebe.

The chaise stopped, startling her. So soon, so soon . . . The carriage door swung open and one of the footmen handed her down to the pavement. When she looked up at her new home, the magnificent house that Mrs. Langdon had brought to her marriage to Roger Darrington, her hand flew to her mouth to stifle her cry of astonishment. Though she had never in her life been in this section of London, Deirdre was almost certain she had seen this magnificent red brick mansion before. But where? Had it been in her dream, her dream of Clive on his wedding day?

Leaving Agnes to see to their luggage, she hurried inside, sweeping past a liveried footman, half-hearing him informing her that the family was in the drawing room, rushed by an open door through which she glimpsed her father, and hurried down a long hall to French doors leading to the side of the house and, her pulses pounding, through those doors onto a stone terrace overlooking a rose garden.

Now she was certain, there could be no doubt, this was the very place she had seen in her dream, the setting where Clive would one day celebrate his marriage, not to her, not to Deirdre Darrington, but to Phoebe Langdon.

With a heavy heart, she reentered the house and made her way with reluctant steps to the drawing room, where she found her father, stepmother, and two stepsisters impatiently awaiting her appearance. The salon was high-ceilinged, an invitingly bright room whose tasteful furnishings and rich carpeting were reflected in the mirrors on the walls. Deirdre recalled seeing more than the usual number of mirrors in the entry and in the hall as well.

"This is my wife, Sybil," Roger Darrington said proudly as he introduced Deirdre to a rather plump matronly woman whose blonde hair owed as much, if not more, to art as it did to nature.

Perhaps an unkind observation, Deirdre told herself, but only the simple truth.

What shall I call her? she wondered, upset that she had failed to consider the matter until now. She could never think of her father's new wife as "Mother," and "Sybil" seemed much too familiar. "Stepmama"? How awkward that sounded. In the end, she settled, albeit hesitantly and uncomfortably, on "Mrs. Darrington."

"Dear Roger," Sybil said, looking fondly up at her new husband, "you led me to expect someone quite different. Your appearance, my dear," she told Deirdre, "comes as rather a surprise, since we expected someone a bit younger. At least, I did." She glanced at her older daughter as though for confirmation.

"Someone *considerably* younger." Phoebe's tone seemed not only to express agreement with her mother, but to accuse her stepfather of purposefully misleading them.

Deirdre took her first thoroughgoing look at the blonde, blue-eyed young lady who was destined to be Clive's bride. I must not stare, she reminded herself, and yet she had difficulty forcing herself to look away. Before this moment she had met only one girl, a seamstress from the village of Hartfield, who she could truthfully have called beautiful. Phoebe now became the second. Her new stepsister was like a painting that entices one to sit hour after hour in silent admiration, a work of art capable of providing unending pleasure to the fortunate viewer.

No wonder Clive had been smitten. Any man would have been.

Phoebe's only flaw, Deirdre finally decided, was a most decided lack of animation, a severe case of the dismals undoubtedly occasioned, Deirdre reminded herself, by worry lest harm should befall Clive Chadbourne in Spain.

"How sorry I am, my dear, if I misled you," Roger Darrington apologized to his wife. "In my defense, let me say I share your surprise, since Deirdre has changed considerably since last I saw her."

Her father seemed to hover near his new wife, attentive to her every word, eager to see her every wish fulfilled. Sybil responded by gazing lovingly up at him or by every now and then reaching out to touch his sleeve or his hand. Was it possible, Deirdre wondered, that older couples—her father was fifty—had much the same feelings as those considerably younger?

"Our new sister has a decidedly Irish look about her," Phoebe said.

Deirdre had the uncomfortable feeling of being on display in front of an unsympathetic audience. "I *am* Irish," she said, "at least, on my mother's side." Make of it what you will, Miss Phoebe Langdon, she added to herself.

Phoebe rolled her eyes ever so slightly, but said nothing.

"And this," Sybil said to Deirdre, "is my other daughter, Alcida, who is two months younger than yourself." She nodded to a young lady who sat

34

with her face lowered as she stroked a white Angora cat curled on her lap. "If only you would stop playing with Beauty, Alcida, and be courteous enough to greet your new sister."

Alcida, whose brown ringlets partially covered her face, looked up at Deirdre with a shy, welcoming smile.

"How many times have I told you to draw your hair back?" her mother asked.

As Alcida readjusted her hair ribbon, Deirdre suppressed a sigh of sympathy, for she saw that the girl's otherwise pretty face was marred by the white scars of the pox. As soon as she recaptured her ringlets, Alcida ducked her head once more.

"I hope and trust," Deirdre said impulsively to Alcida, "that you and I will become the best of friends."

Alcida glanced up at her with mixed surprise and hope, but before she could reply, Deirdre's father said, with the easy confidence of ignorance, "Of course you will be friends with Alcida, and with Phoebe as well, since you are now, after all, sisters."

Later, after being shown to her room and following a formal tea, Mrs. Darrington proposed that the three sisters stroll in the rose garden "to further your acquaintance with one another." They had scarcely walked down the stone steps from the terrace before Phoebe began to quiz Deirdre.

"Prior to his leaving London," she said, "dear Clive told me of his intention to stop at Chadbourne House on his way to Portsmouth. Did he happen to visit you while he was there?"

Deirdre's face reddened as she recalled her distress at the news he had brought to East Sussex, the news of his betrothal. "Oh, yes, Father wrote saying Clive was coming and he did." Flustered, she decided that the less said about his humiliating visit, the better.

"You exhibit such a vivid blush at the mention of Clive's name," Phoebe said sharply.

"You see," Alcida put in tentatively, "we imagined Clive visiting someone who was considerably younger."

"That is not true at all," Phoebe corrected her, "since we were made aware of your exact age by your father. In listening to him and to Clive, however, we received an impression of a young miss who was more of an annoyance than anything else."

"Yes," Alcida said, "a rather childish girl."

"If only you would refrain from constantly echoing my words," Phoebe told her sister. Glancing at Deirdre, she smiled, but her smile, Deirdre noted, contained not a trace of good humor. "I sometimes refer to Alcida as Miss Ifonly," Phoebe said, "because everyone who knows her is constantly saying 'If only' you would do this, Alcida, or 'If only' you would do that, Alcida. And quite rightly so."

Deirdre glanced at Alcida, who quickly lowered her head, but not before Deirdre detected the glint of tears in the younger girl's eyes. As for herself, Deirdre frowned in uncomfortable embarrassment

36

at Phoebe's unnecessary cruelty. Unobtrusively, she reached for Alcida's hand and squeezed it in silent sympathy.

"I find it rather discomfiting," Phoebe went on, "to discover that someone other than myself was the last person to see Clive before his departure for the Peninsula. When he left here, he should have journeyed directly to Portsmouth without stopping in East Sussex."

Deirdre could think of no adequate response to Phoebe's novel notion of what constituted fidelity. And she certainly did not intend to protest that she and Clive had been friends for many years.

"However that might be," Phoebe said, "I, for one, have no intention of dwelling on lapses of the past." She brightened slightly. "On Saturday week, Deirdre, we are all invited to a ball at Lord Harmon's to welcome his son Edward Fox, Marquess of Lounsbury—a courtesy title, of course—his only son, by the bye, and therefore heir to Harmon Hall, home after a year spent in the Canadian wilderness. Edward is quite handsome."

"And rather wicked," Alcida added in a low voice edged with both fear and fascination. "He is reputed to be a rake."

"The tittle-tattle in town has it," Phoebe went on, ignoring her sister's comment, "that Edward returns to England in search of a suitable wife." She glanced meaningfully at Deirdre. "Though I suggest you refrain from raising your hopes too high, since I rather expect he will settle on someone from the *ton* with impeccable English antecedents and a fitting position in society. And I feel certain he must be well aware that, while my mother had no reason to marry for money, the same cannot be said for your father."

Conquering her rising anger with difficulty, Deirdre vowed not to give Phoebe the satisfaction of nettling her into making a scathing reply.

"I fear I shall have a perfectly dreadful time at the Harmon ball," Phoebe went on. "I shall not be able to venture onto the floor, no matter how many times I happen to be invited, since my affections are committed to one who is honorably serving his country in distant lands." She sighed. "Although Edward is said to be a wonderful dancer and I love to dance—there is, in fact, nothing I enjoy more—I shall be forced to sit and suffer in silence."

From the little she had learned of Phoebe, Deirdre considered that while her new stepsister might suffer, she was unlikely to do so in silence. But again she said nothing.

"I suppose," Phoebe went on, "I will have to become a second Alcida, a wallflower who spends her time at balls chatting with her mother and the other older ladies while hiding her face behind her fan."

Alcida drew in a sharp breath; she seemed to be attempting to gather enough courage to enable her to lash back at her sister, but instead of answering, she whirled around and ran up the stone steps to the terrace and on into the house.

Deirdre's simmering anger finally boiled over.

"You should be ashamed," she told Phoebe, "to speak to Alcida in such a humbling way."

"What right have you to dictate what I say to my own sister?" Phoebe demanded. "Is it possible everyone in this house except myself is reluctant to hear the truth? Are you all afraid? And I thought the Irish were fearless in their primitive way."

Deirdre eyed her steadily. "You might like to think all of us are afraid," she said, her voice low and intense, "and you might succeed in flustering Alcida, but you will never intimidate me. *Never.*"

Phoebe sniffed and turned away, folding her arms and staring off into the distance. Deirdre, her hands clenched at her sides in anger, swung about and followed Alcida into the house.

As she hurried past the library, she glanced in at the open door and saw the younger girl's image reflected in the looking glass over the fireplace. Alcida, who had been sitting on a couch, playing listlessly with a kitten, looked up and saw Deirdre at almost the same time. She immediately lowered her head into her hands.

When Deirdre came to sit beside her, Alcida, without raising her head, said, "This house has so many looking glasses. I counted them once and found there were forty-three. I hate them, every last one of them, all forty-three of them. Wherever I look, I see myself."

Deirdre took Alcida's hands and drew them away from her face. "You have such pretty eyes," she said, "and such lustrous hair."

Alcida shook her head hopelessly. "I know what

I look like and you know what I look like, and so does Phoebe, and everyone else who meets me." She nestled the kitten in her arms. "Thank you for taking my part with my sister," she said, "but you must not let Phoebe distress you. That is the way she is."

"Phoebe has a very sharp tongue."

"I came down with the smallpox when I was nine," Alcida said. "For a long time afterward, Phoebe could hardly bear to look at me because of my scars, they distressed her so. Not only that, I think she was angry with me for getting sick. We were all quarantined and Phoebe had to postpone her birthday party."

"No one falls ill on purpose."

"No, and Phoebe's not the way she is on purpose, either. Sometimes, I admit, she speaks without giving thought to the harm her words might do. I often wonder if being unhappy makes her say all those hurtful things."

"Unhappy? Phoebe?"

The notion startled Deirdre into speechlessness. With her surpassing beauty, how could Phoebe possibly be unhappy? Besides, and more importantly, she had the most felicitous of futures to look forward to, since she would soon become Clive's wife. Alcida's explanation, though demonstrating her kindness in seeking an excuse for her sister, was nothing less than preposterous.

"She *is* unhappy, you know," Alcida insisted, as she placed the kitten on the carpet and then touched Deirdre's arm with tentative fingers.

"When Phoebe failed to receive a voucher for Almack's, she cried for two days. As for myself—" She sighed. "If only you could help us, Deirdre, if only you would try."

Deirdre put her hand over Alcida's—reassuringly she hoped—all the while wondering if she could even help herself.

*Deirdre rode across a dark and silent plain. Death stalked her and she was afraid, more afraid than she had ever been before. Without warning, a great light flashed near her, followed by a roar louder than the loudest thunder. Another flash of light, closer than before, almost blinded her, and there came another roar and another flash, this time closer still, threateningly close, the air around her becoming acrid, the taste of fear sour in her mouth . . .*

*A flash brighter than all the rest stunned her, hurled her backward. She was falling, falling, and then—oblivion. She opened her eyes and reached out, and when her fingers scrabbled on loose earth, she realized she had been thrown from her horse to the ground.*

*She was no longer alone, for from all around her came the piteous cries of wounded men calling for water, calling for help. Pain throbbed in her temple, and when she put an exploring hand to her forehead she felt a sticky substance. Snatching her hand away, she realized she had touched blood, her blood . . .*

Deirdre sat up in bed. The chamber was dark. It was only a dream, she assured herself. There was no blood; she was unharmed. Why, then, did this searing pain not cease, a pain so intense it precluded thought, a pain that forced her to put her hand to her forehead and made her close her eyes in a vain attempt to seek relief?

As the throbbing slowly eased, the pain receding, a different kind of pain pierced her heart. Of a sudden, she realized what her dream meant. Clive! She knew with a dreadful certainty he had been hurt, grievously hurt. If only she could be with him to tend his wounds. But she could not.

There was nothing she could do to help him except clasp her hands and pray.

# Chapter Four

"Our carriage is ready," Alcida said from the doorway to Deirdre's bedchamber.

Deirdre nodded, settling her Chinese shawl over her shoulders before leaving the room. As they walked to the top of the curving staircase, she asked, "Where is Phoebe? Did she change her mind at the last moment about going to Lord Harmon's ball?"

Alcida glanced right and left before saying, in a confidential whisper, "If she had her way, Phoebe would be the first to arrive at the ball and the last to leave."

"Alcida! Deirdre!"

They turned to see Phoebe motioning to them from the doorway of her room.

"You must come here at once and look," Phoebe insisted. "Both of you."

When they entered the bedchamber, Phoebe was posed between a cheval glass and a looking glass on the wall. "How many Phoebes can you count?" she asked.

Standing beside her, Deirdre saw their images almost endlessly reflected back and forth between the two mirrors. How beautiful Phoebe looked, Deirdre thought, in her exquisite lawn gown of light blue, the color perfectly matching her eyes.

The gown featured three satin bands and a fringe of sky blue just above the hem; blue satin braid decorated both the square neck of her bodice and the bands of her puffed sleeves. Her light blue velvet headband—decorated with small white roses—contrasted prettily with her blond curls.

"I count eight Phoebes," Deirdre said, "and each new image seems even lovelier than the one before." It was no more than the truth.

"La," Phoebe said with a satisfied smile, "we really must leave, Mother will be most impatient. And as for your father—" But still she lingered to admire her reflections in the two glasses, first touching her hair, then opening and fluttering her fan.

"Your gown flatters you," she said, glancing at Deirdre. "If only you could do something with your hair to allow the curls to fall properly in a graceful disarray over your brow."

A hasty look in the mirror told Deirdre that her green satin hair ribbon was, as usual, fighting a losing battle to contain her riotous red curls. She did like her gown, though. The dress, of French cambric muslin, was decorated with narrow emerald-green braid at the high waist, along the bow in the back, and just above the hem. The green braid outlining the scoop neck of her bodice accentuated the pale skin of her shoulders and neck. The gown might flatter her, but nothing, she was aware, would ever turn her into a beauty like Phoebe.

With a last lingering glance into the mirror, Phoebe turned and led the way along the hall and down the curving staircase. As they settled into the carriage beside the obviously impatient elder Darringtons, Phoebe said, "We were admiring one another's gowns."

Sybil smiled affectionately at her elder daughter. "All three of you will turn heads tonight," she predicted, nodding at Deirdre.

Deirdre, though aware Sybil favored Phoebe, was surprised and gratified by having her stepmother notice her.

"I warrant I shall be quite bored," Phoebe said, "since I have absolutely no intention of dancing. Even if Edward begs me for a dance, I shall refuse the honor despite his being our host."

Deirdre listened to the wheels of the carriage rattling over the cobbles while Phoebe listed the sacrifices she was forced to make because of her devotion to Clive Chadbourne. Closing her ears to Phoebe's words, she allowed her thoughts to roam, recalling the dispatches in the *Morning Post* recounting a great victory by Lord Wellington at Vittoria in Spain and reporting that the hated French were in retreat eastward toward the Pyrenees. Beyond the Pyrenees lay France.

There had been, to her consternation, no word as yet either from or about Clive.

If her dreams were truly prophetic, Deirdre assured herself for the hundredth time, Clive had been wounded but, thank God, the dream had shown he was alive. He would, she hoped, be coming back to England, perhaps soon. To Deirdre, his well-being was all-important; the fact that he was returning not to her but to Phoebe mattered little in comparison.

Having almost convinced herself that Clive was safe, she vowed to try her best to enjoy herself at the Harmons' ball. Since this was her first fledgling step into London society, into the world of the *ton,* she felt a certain trepidation mingled with the excitement of anticipation.

As their carriage slowed, Deirdre glanced from the window at the other carriages waiting in a long line ahead of them, all waiting to leave their passengers at the front steps of the Harmon mansion. The great house, bulking massively behind six imposing white columns, blazed with lights, torches outside and lamps within.

At last they stepped down from their carriage and were ushered into a reception room where, after still another wait, they were announced and met their hosts, Lord and Lady Harmon and their son Edward, the Marquess of Lounsbury. For some reason Deirdre had expected Edward to be a dark, brooding gentleman with the disdainful smile of a Lord Byron; he was not. Of middle height and fair, he had a warm smile that brightened a face tanned by the sun.

Phoebe, Deirdre noted, seemed transformed in the presence of Lord Harmon and his heir. No longer pouting or sullen, she smiled engagingly up at the two men, her blue eyes sparkling with pleasure.

Leaving their hosts, the Darrington party walked slowly down the grand staircase into the ballroom, the lively music from an orchestra on a low balcony swirling about them, the murmur from an untold number of conversations rising and falling, the glittering light of scores of candles reflecting from the hundreds of lusters in the chandeliers as well as from the dazzling jewels of the women.

Soon after they had settled themselves in chairs some distance from the dance floor, Phoebe opened her fan, raised it to shield her face, and whispered to Deirdre and Alcida, "I do believe Edward is walking in our direction. If he should ask me for the honor of a dance, not that I expect he will, I must refuse him, of course, because I have vowed to be true to dear Clive."

Deirdre glanced from the corner of her eye. Yes, without a doubt, Edward was making his way toward them, nodding and smiling to his other guests as he threaded his way between the chairs. He bowed to Roger, murmured a compliment to Sybil, and paid his respects to Deirdre and Phoebe before turning to Alcida.

"Will you do me the honor, Miss Alcida?" he asked.

Bemused, Alcida stared up at him. She dropped her fan and awkwardly bent down to retrieve it. "I really—" she began, but before she could utter another word, Edward took her hand in his, drew her to her feet, and declaring his surprised pleasure at the mildness of the English spring after the bitter cold of the Canadian winter, escorted her to the floor.

A short time later, as Deirdre was strolling with Sybil while sipping a glass of cold punch, Alcida joined them. When Sybil turned away to speak to a friend, Alcida confided in a whisper, "Edward was quite charming and not in the least wicked. He complimented me on my gown." She wore a pale pink lawn, simple yet attractive.

"As well he should," Deirdre said. "Was that the sum and substance of his conversation?"

Alcida smiled uncertainly. "He also expressed a great affection for volcanoes."

"Volcanoes? What an unusual topic for a ballroom conversation."

"While in Canada—he was there for almost two years at the behest of his father—he explored the site of what everyone claimed was an extinct volcano. Edward, however, refused to believe the volcano to be completely dormant. He pictured to me, in quite graphic and at times rather frightening terms, the molten rock and hot lava seething beneath the surface of the earth, only awaiting its opportunity to break through in a violent and fiery eruption, spewing a torrent of molten rock into the air. All in all, I found the notion to be quite exhilarating."

"Shhh," Deirdre cautioned, "your newfound friend from the Colonies is fast approaching."

Edward bowed to them both and asked Deirdre to dance. "My pleasure, Lord Lounsbury," she told him, pleasantly surprised to discover she was not nearly so nervous as she had feared she might be.

"Not Lord Lounsbury—Edward, if you please," he said, as he led her through the crush to where the next set was forming. "We should become allies, Miss Darrington, you and I," he murmured, "since we are both strangers to the *ton*." When he glanced upward from her eyes to her head, she wondered if her hair had completely escaped confinement, as it was inclined to do.

"Allies? Are we two then engaged in a war that I know nothing of?"

"We are indeed. The *ton* is the site of a whole series of small wars, young gentlemen arrayed against young ladies, young ladies against gentlemen, the mushrooms striving to surpass those next above them on society's scale, the matrons with marriageable daughters waging an unceasing campaign to capture all eligible bachelors, the indebted fighting a rearguard action against the moneylenders who hold their chits, the evangelists seeking to recruit the sinners while the sinners attempt to make prey of everyone else. The list of combatants is endless."

Deirdre smiled, now almost completely at ease with him. "You make me wonder where you and I fit into this contentious scene."

The music began and the dance separated them before he could answer.

"For the moment, having newly arrived, we are able to stand apart," he said as they came together again, "while we either cheer on the contestants or commiserate with them. In another month, that will be impossible for we, too, shall be engaged in one or another of the battles."

"Before I enter into an agreement with you," she said, "I would certainly insist on references attesting to your reliability as an ally, my lord."

"Call me Edward, please." He glanced around the room. "If only there were someone here who could speak favorably of me. Alas, there is not one soul who knows me as I truly am."

"Although there are many who believe they do?"

"Rumor has it they do. Pray tell me, Deirdre, what does the *ton* say of me?" Again they were separated.

She quite enjoyed the challenge of conversing with Lord Lounsbury—no, Edward, Deirdre decided. Perhaps the stories about him were the malicious exaggerations of the envious, perhaps they were completely false. She trusted her own judgment more than any tittle-tattle.

"I have heard two tales about you," she said when they came together. "The first is that a reputation for being rather wicked follows you from Canada. The other claims you returned to England with the intention of seeking a wife."

He stared at her, then threw his head back and laughed. "I quite enjoy your refreshing frankness," he said. "The trait is in short supply here; in fact, a tradesman could reap a fortune by importing candor to Londontown and peddling it in Mayfair."

"Would you be a buyer or a seller, my lord — Edward?"

"I possess more than enough candor to suit my needs. I may lie to you, but if I do, you should take it as a compliment, since one of my rules in life is to lie only to beautiful women. As for the stories you hear claiming I seek a wife and those assailing my character, one of them is true, the other false."

The set ended and they left the floor to wend their way through the crush to the room where a variety of food and drink was arrayed on buffet tables.

"And which of the two stories is true and which false?" Deirdre asked him.

"Alas, Deirdre, that must remain my secret. In my experience, any man or woman without at least one closely held secret is extremely boring. As for myself, I acknowledge having more than one." He glanced at her. "And I suspect *you* do as well."

She started to shake her head, to deny having any secrets at all, but then she blushed. Clive, she thought, my love for Clive is my secret, a secret that must remain locked in my heart forever.

To distract Edward's attention, she said, "Let me guess which story about you is true and which false. In my opinion, you believe yourself to be rather wicked, but would profess to having no desire whatsoever to be married." When he smiled, she went on, "I think the opposite might actually be true, that in fact you are not at all wicked, but in your heart of hearts would like to be married."

"Most people of my acquaintance, and particularly young ladies, make a habit of believing what they want to believe." As he handed her a glass of punch, his gaze once again centered on her hair.

"Is my hair in such complete disarray?" she asked, frowning.

"Not at all. While in the Canadian wilderness, I lived for a time among the Indians and your hair reminds me of a legend common among the Iroquois of eastern Canada. The story tells of a beautiful red-haired maiden who arrives from across the great Eastern Sea and becomes what we might call a goddess, a woman they referred to as their 'golden princess of the dawn.' "

"In all my reading about the American Indians, I have never encountered such a story."

He nodded. "I would be greatly surprised if you had, since I must confess the tale was a figment of my imagination, a legend the Iroquois should adopt but, alas, have not. The truth is that your flaming hair intrigues me, reminds me of something, but I know not what."

Raising her glass of punch to her lips, she looked at him over the rim. "A volcano in full eruption, perhaps," she said with seeming innocence.

He blinked and his lips twisted in the semblance of a smile. "Much as I would like to," he said, "I dare not pursue the comparison. Not from any fear of where it might lead, but because I observe your father bearing down on us with the intent, I expect, of rescuing his princess of the dawn from the evil stranger. With this crush to impede him, however, we have time to slip through that door to the garden. I can assure you there are superb vistas to be enjoyed from our gazebo."

"At this time of night?"

"There are those who maintain that the pleasures of the gazebo in the moonlight surpass those of the more prosaic daylight hours."

"Perhaps another time."

"May I consider that a—?"

Before she could reply, Roger Darrington came up to them and greeted Edward civilly but immediately took Deirdre by the arm and, with a nod to Edward, led her away.

"A promise?" Edward called after her.

Deirdre looked over her shoulder and smiled without indicating whether her answer would be a yes or a no.

She glanced at her father's stern face. "Lord Lounsbury is, I understand, considered something of a rake."

"Harrumph," her father said. He appeared to debate whether to elaborate on this noncommittal remark. "Stories have circulated," he said at last, "vague yet disturbing stories having to do with his conduct while in Canada. I never inquired as to the details nor, I trust, will the occasion ever arise that may force me to do so." He looked past her. "Ah, here comes Aldrich to ask you to dance, I expect. Splendid chap, young Aldrich . . ."

Deirdre danced with James Aldrich, with

Charles Hampton, with Arthur Scofield, and with a succession of other young men, their names and faces finally blurring in her mind. Alcida, she noticed with satisfaction, also had her share of partners.

Still later, when Deirdre was sitting with her father, Alcida came to her, all agog, and whispered in her ear. "You must see for yourself," she said. "Will we ever live down the gossip?"

Excusing herself, Deirdre followed her stepsister to the edge of the ballroom floor and watched with a puzzled frown as Alcida stood on tiptoe to scan the dancers. "I saw her dancing," Alcida said in shocked tones, "but now she has quite vanished."

"Who was dancing? Who has vanished?"

"Why, Phoebe, of course. After insisting she never would, she was dancing with Edward and, worse, she appeared to be enjoying herself immensely. How could she? Were all her protestations of faithfulness to Clive untrue?"

"You may be judging her too hastily, Alcida. Is there anything so terribly wrong in dancing a single dance with Edward? He *is* our host."

"Where can she be?" Alcida asked. Sighing in frustration, she turned from the dance floor. "Would you have danced with Edward if you were betrothed to Clive?" Alcida asked, as they slowly made their way back to rejoin the elder Darringtons.

Would she? Deirdre asked herself. No, of course not. "Everyone is different," she said.

Alcida gasped and clutched Deirdre's arm. When Deirdre followed her gaze, she saw Phoebe slipping into the room through the door to the garden. Closing the door, Phoebe glanced guiltily about her, appearing both flushed and flustered. Edward was nowhere to be seen.

How strange, Deirdre thought. For a moment she wondered whether Phoebe and Edward might have been enjoying some of the promised pleasures of the Harmon gazebo by moonlight, but just as quickly she banished the uncharitable notion from her mind. No woman betrothed to Clive, she assured herself, could possibly be even slightly interested in any other man.

They arrived home as the first rays of the sun were brightening the eastern sky over the rooftops. After opening the door for them, Morland handed Roger Darrington a letter. "Dr. Leicester called earlier," he said, "and was most anxious you receive this."

Frowning, Roger opened the letter at once. "Good news," he said, "not bad. And more for your ears, Phoebe, than mine. Dr. Leicester writes that word has reached Clive Chadbourne's father that Clive arrives home within the fortnight."

# Chapter Five

"We should plan a very simple affair," Phoebe said at dinner a few days later, "to welcome dear Clive home from Spain and to show him our gratitude for his heroic sacrifices for England."

The day after the Harmons' ball Phoebe received a brief letter from Clive, posted, as he said, in haste from Portsmouth, giving the date of his return to London. Deirdre was relieved to learn that he made no mention of being wounded. Her dream, undoubtedly prompted by her fear for his safety, had thus proved false.

"Yes," Sybil agreed, "an intimate gathering of the family, perhaps a tea where we all will have an opportunity to hear Clive describe his experiences as a member of Lord Wellington's command."

"Dr. Leicester is such a close friend of Clive's," Alcida put in, "perhaps he should be invited."

Deirdre glanced in surprise at Alcida, who rarely ventured an opinion of any sort, but found her staring down at her plate.

Roger Darrington nodded his agreement. "We must remember," he said, "how gracious it was of

Lord and Lady Harmon to invite us all to the ball that was also, in effect, a welcoming celebration to mark his son's return from Canada. Since we intend to celebrate Clive's return from Spain, they might consider us remiss if we fail to return the compliment."

"In any event, Edward should be invited," Phoebe said quickly—perhaps too quickly, Deirdre thought, "since he and Clive have always been such good friends."

"If Lord Harmon and his family are invited," Sybil said, "we can hardly fail to invite their cousins, Mr. and Mrs. Aldrich, and their son. Not to mention Mrs. Aldrich's sister, Mrs. Hampton, as well as her husband and their two lovely daughters."

Phoebe nodded. "Clive will undoubtedly insist that I play a few selections on the pianoforte during the party," she said, "for he dotes on my playing and we should provide some suitable entertainment for our guests. If I perform, Elizabeth Hampton will be certain to encourage someone to ask her to sing. She *is* rather talented in her untutored way."

"I do believe," Roger said, "that our guests will deem it the height of inhospitality if we fail to serve dinner. A musical evening, as you suggest, Phoebe, followed by a simple repast, would be a most appropriate celebration in honor of young Chadbourne, a welcome befitting a hero of the war against Napoleon."

"And I, for one," Phoebe said, "would love to have dancing during the evening after my many weeks of sitting and watching others dance. Nothing elaborate, certainly, perhaps only a single fiddler. Dear Clive so enjoys dancing, and this party is, after all, in his honor."

"Might we not," Deirdre asked, "be planning too elaborate a party? Clive could well be fatigued from traveling; he might enjoy a quiet gathering on his first evening home."

"If we were living in the country," Phoebe said, "I would agree, but in London we do things differently, Deirdre, quite differently."

Deirdre started to reply in anger, thought better of it, and sank down in her chair with a sigh of resignation. During the next hour, as the plans for the party were discussed and rediscussed and then discussed again, she said nothing more.


The following days passed slowly for Deirdre, her sense of anticipation growing, but along with her eagerness to see Clive again came an unease, a foreboding, a fear that something might be amiss.

At last the evening of the homecoming party arrived. The "simple affair" had, to the professed surprise of everyone in the Darrington household with the exception of Deirdre, mushroomed into a musical evening followed by dancing followed by an elaborate dinner for more than thirty guests.

The first of these guests, Edward Fox and Dr. Vincent Leicester, arrived an hour before Clive was expected.

"Have either of you seen dear Clive as yet?" Phoebe asked them.

The doctor, a stocky young man with curly blond

hair, shook his head. "He was to arrive at the Harmon townhouse this morning and come directly here after a brief visit with his father." Noticing Alcida playing patience at the card table, he drew up a chair, sat across from her, and challenged her to a two-handed game, a challenge she accepted at once.

When Phoebe began an animated conversation with Edward about the doings of mutual friends, Deirdre excused herself and walked outside to the terrace. Ill-at-ease — still wondering if holding this rather grandiose party was a mistake, disturbed by Phoebe's all-too-evident delight in Edward's company, and wanting to see Clive again, yet strangely fearful — she stood for long minutes looking down at the profusion of red and white roses in the garden as the brisk wind tugged fretfully at her hair.

"You appear pensive."

Startled, she looked over her shoulder and saw Edward watching her from the doorway. Walking across the terrace, he came to stand at her side. When he saw her glance back at the house, he said, "I found myself at liberty when Miss Langdon's mother required Phoebe's advice on a matter of grave import having to do, I believe, with the seating arrangements for the dinner."

Uncertain whether to be relieved or annoyed that Edward had interrupted her unhappy musings, Deirdre did not reply, and for a time they stood looking down at the rose garden in silence.

"Dr. Leicester informed me," Edward said finally, "that you and Clive have been country friends for a number of years."

Deirdre glanced at him, but he gave no sign his

remark was anything more than an idle conversational gambit. "Clive spent his summers near my grandmother's home in East Sussex," she said, "where I grew up after the death of my mother."

"You must be better acquainted with him than I am, then, since I know him only casually."

"We are, as you say, friends," she told him, at the same time recalling Phoebe's assertion that a close friendship existed between the two men. Phoebe must have been misinformed.

Again neither spoke for a time, and again it was Edward who broke the silence. "Have you ever noticed," he asked, "how often men, and women as well, for that matter, often spend considerable time and energy in the pursuit of the unattainable?"

"Do you refer to someone in particular?" she asked. Could he be hinting that he had an interest in Phoebe, she wondered, who he well knew was betrothed to another?

"No, I was merely thinking aloud, a habit I acquired in the wilds of Canada, where I spent untold days with no company but my own. It occurred to me that while one of the small tragedies of life is failing to get what you seek, it can be a great tragedy to succeed in getting it."

She started to object, to dispute him, but then she frowned, admitting to herself that in some cases he might well be right.

"Pray pay no heed to my musings," he said with a smile. "Some nights I sit into the late hours with my brandy and soda, perfecting enigmatic remarks intended to astound and amaze the young ladies of my acquaintance."

Young ladies such as Phoebe, Deirdre told herself. She could understand why Phoebe might find Edward fascinating, his wealth and social position aside, but she could not fathom how she could allow herself to flirt with him while awaiting Clive's return.

Edward glanced at her, seemed about to speak, paused, then said, "I have fashioned a small gift for my young nephew Ned," he told her.

She detected a hesitancy in his speech, an unexpected tentativeness. Was it reluctance? Certainly it could not be trepidation. What, then?

"I wonder if you would be so kind," he said, "as to assist me in ascertaining whether my gift performs as it should."

"Assist you here and now?" she asked, her curiosity piqued.

"Now, yes, but certainly not here. Pray come with me."

He offered her his arm and, after a second or two of hesitation, she nodded and walked with him from the terrace into the garden and from there through a gate to the walkway in front of the Darrington house. He nodded toward an open carriage.

When she drew back, he smiled and said, "Fear not, Deirdre, I have no plans to spirit you away to my gazebo."

Despite herself, Deirdre smiled. "What then, sir, *do* you intend?"

"All will soon be revealed."

Turning from her, he shouted, "Cunningham!" A footman's head popped up from the rear of the carriage. "Come along, Cunningham, if you will," Edward called to him, "and bring Ned's gift." Looking at Deirdre as they walked on, he said, "You have my word we shall go only as far as the square across the street."

"The gate is kept locked."

"Ah, but since most such London parks are locked, I had the foresight to bring this from the Darrington house." He took a large black key from his pocket and held it aloft.

As they crossed the street, a rabbit woman walked past them crying her wares, "Rabbits, rabbits, who will buy my rabbits?" She carried a long pole over her right shoulder with dead rabbits suspended from the front, and wild fowl and a basket from the back.

"She probably carries pigeons in the basket," Edward said as he unlocked the gate and held it open for her. After entering the small park, Deirdre looked behind her and saw Cunningham, a short and slender young man, hurrying after them, clutching a red kite with a tail of white rags, a kite almost as tall as Cunningham himself.

Edward intended to have her fly the kite with him. Was it her fate, Deirdre wondered, to have all young gentlemen treat her as though she were still a child? Clive had often called her his younger sister; now Edward sought to amuse her by flying a kite in the park. And yet the kite reminded her, happily, of being a carefree child, of roaming the fields with Clive.

"The park is somewhat small for kite flying," Deirdre noted, ruefully realizing her rose-sprigged muslin gown was not entirely suitable for such an adventure.

"We shall manage quite well." Taking the kite in one hand and twine wrapped around a small stick in the other, he thanked Cunningham and gestured his footman back to the carriage.

"Determine the direction of the wind," he told Deirdre, "by first wetting your finger and—"

"I am well aware of the method," she said, smiling as she held her moistened forefinger above her head. "The wind is from the west," she told him.

"If you would be so kind." He handed her the kite and, as she held it by its wooden frame, he started to walk into the breeze, unwinding the twine as he went. "When I call out," he said, "release the kite."

He began to run away from her; he called to her, called her name; she released the kite and watched as it rose steadily only to suddenly and swiftly veer to the right and fall, hitting the ground with a worrisome *crack*.

"Damnation," Edward muttered, as he knelt to examine the damage.

Taking a piece of string from his pocket, he cut it with a knife and bound and tied the broken rib. "We must try again," he told Deirdre.

He handed her the kite, walked away, and began to run; she let go and watched the kite rising, soaring up, up, up, to the top of the trees in the park, higher than the highest building, up into the pale blue of the sky, Edward laughing with delight at his success while Deirdre, a child once more, clapped her hands.

He came to her and bowed slightly as he presented her with the stick wrapped round with twine. Holding the stick in both hands, she felt the kite tugging as it sought to break free of all restraint. She closed her eyes, imagining that Clive stood beside her, that they were together once more, young and happy.

When Edward spoke, she was jolted from her reverie. "We seem to have an audience of one." He nodded to the opposite side of the park, where a small, begrimed boy of nine or ten peered at them through the iron bars of the fence.

When Edward approached him, the boy turned as though to flee. Deirdre heard Edward speak quietly to him — he was too far away for her to understand the words — and the boy stopped and reluctantly returned to the fence. Edward stood on one of the lower iron railings, reached over the spiked top, and lifted the boy into the park.

"He tells me his name is Floyd," Edward said, when they came to Deirdre, who stood holding the twine. "His mother happens to be the rabbit woman, and the boy is waiting for her to sell the rest of her wares. I enticed Floyd into the park by offering him the chance to fly the kite."

Taking the twine from Deirdre, he handed it to the eager boy and stood beside him as Floyd first brought the kite lower and then allowed it to soar higher than ever. How patient he was with the boy, Deirdre told herself, perhaps she should reserve judgment about Edward and his supposed wickedness. He seemed to be a man of contradictions.

"Would you like to have a kite like this?" Edward asked the boy.

When Floyd nodded eagerly, Edward placed a hand on his shoulder and said, "Then you do. As of this moment, the kite is yours."

Floyd, still clutching the stick with both hands, eyed Edward with the suspicion of one accustomed to being betrayed.

"He suspects I have some ulterior and probably dastardly motive." Edward turned from the boy, taking Deirdre's arm and escorting her to the gate. "The best way to convince him otherwise is to leave him in sole possession of the kite."

"How very kind you are." Which was only the truth, she told herself.

"Did it occur to you I may have given the lad the kite merely to alter what I suspect is your poor opinion of me? So you would possess a wee bit of evidence as to my true character to weigh in the balance against your rather wary assessment of me?"

"And is that why you gave Floyd the kite? Merely to impress me? I find that difficult to believe."

"As it happens, impressing you was but a secondary consideration. I took a liking to this boy; I wanted to do something for him. My nephew can wait another day or two while I fashion a second kite. Besides, this kite was damaged." Edward stopped and looked at her, saying, "May I ask you a what-if question?"

Without waiting for her reply, he went on. "That boy we just left in the park, the lad Floyd . . . what would you do, Deirdre, if your father came to you holding Floyd by the hand and said, 'I want you to help me raise this boy"? Recognizing that here we have a youngster with none of the social graces, whose every word brands him as poor and untutored, whose pallid appearance suggests a susceptibility to disease."

"What a strange question. And what an unlikely thing to happen!" She studied him, but his face offered no clue to his reason for asking.

"Admittedly strange," he said. "You need not, of course, answer."

"But I shall answer. I would do exactly as my father asked," Deirdre said. "Not only because he wanted me to do it, but because I believe that what a boy—nay, any child—becomes is more important than what he once was or what he happens to be now."

Edward nodded. "I more or less expected that would be your reply," he said, without indicating whether it pleased or disappointed him.

Before she could ask him to explain himself, a carriage rumbled past them, slowing and coming to a stop in front of the Darrington house. Deirdre drew in her breath, forgetting Edward as a tall, dark-haired young man stepped down from the carriage, slowly climbed the steps to the front door, and disappeared inside.

Clive! At long last, Clive had returned home from the war.

# Chapter Six

Once she saw Clive, Deirdre hurried toward the house after him, abandoning all else. Only when Edward called her name did she belatedly realize her impulsiveness was most impolite. She paused, waiting for him to join her.

"Your eagerness to greet your stepsister's fiancé, the returning cavalry hero, is most commendable," Edward said in an annoyed, almost angry tone, "boding well for harmony between the Chadbourne and Darrington households following the wedding."

Although nettled by what she considered his unprovoked and unseemly sarcasm, Deirdre answered calmly, "Months ago I dreamed Clive had been wounded during the fighting in Spain. My dream was so real I felt compelled to hasten after him to assure myself he was all right."

"He certainly appears to be in fine fettle," Edward said as he offered her his arm.

After a slight hesitation, she allowed him to escort her into the house. She might have resented Edward's veiled reprimand, but he was, after all, correct. Phoebe must be the first to greet Clive.

As they left the entry and began walking along the hall, Deirdre saw Clive standing to one side of the archway leading to the music room where the guests had gathered. Since the hum of conversation from the room continued unabated, she assumed he had yet to make his presence known.

Clive, unaware of Edward and Deirdre's approach, squared his shoulders and stepped into the center of the archway, stopping there with his hands clasped behind his back. The talk and laughter inside the room subsided and after a moment ceased altogether.

A woman screamed. Clive strode into the room, disappearing from Deirdre's sight.

Edward hurried after Clive with Deirdre a step behind. As she paused beneath the arch, she saw Phoebe lying on the flowered couch, her face ashen and her eyes closed. Clive was kneeling at her side, holding both of her hands in his. Deirdre gasped. There was a vivid red welt extending from just above Clive's left eye to his sideburns.

Her dream! In her dream she had seen him wounded in battle . . . just as earlier she had foreseen the celebration of his wedding on the terrace of this very house. Edward, she noticed, had turned to stare at her, undoubtedly recalling her description of her dream, his gaze skeptical while at the same time puzzled.

"Dr. Leicester!" Sybil cried.

The doctor stepped forward to grip Clive's shoulder, urging him to stand aside. Leaning over Phoebe, Dr. Leicester waved smelling salts back and forth under her nose. Phoebe sneezed and opened her eyes. She stared up at the doctor and then looked at Clive, her stricken gaze fixing on his wound.

"Oh, dear God," Phoebe murmured, her hands flying up to cover her face. "What a shock, what a terrible, terrible shock."

"I should have warned you, Phoebe," Clive said with a rueful sigh. He glanced about him. "Warned all of you." Again he came to kneel at Phoebe's side, taking her hands in his. "I said nothing, my dearest, because I wanted you to see for yourself I was safe."

Safe, perhaps, Deirdre told herself, but hardly unchanged. Although, in her eyes, despite his injury, he was still the most handsome man she had ever seen or ever hoped to see, her searching gaze found no trace of the exuberant Clive who had left England only months before. That young man had been left behind, somewhere in Spain, to be replaced by this older, more somber Clive.

As Phoebe slowly sat up, her mother, who had been hovering nervously nearby, looked around the room at her guests and said, "Perhaps we should all let Phoebe and Clive have a quiet time together . . . to allow them to become reacquainted."

"No!" Phoebe cried, shaking her head, her eyes wide and frightened. Drawing in a deep breath, she quieted herself. "Dear, dear Mama," she said with a wan smile, "I assure you, I have quite recovered. I planned to welcome dear Clive home by playing one of his favorite songs, and now I shall do just that."

She stood and, taking Clive's arm, allowed him to lead her to the pianoforte without, Deirdre noted, once glancing at him. Though unnaturally pale, Phoebe looked quite lovely, Deirdre thought, in her blue muslin gown whose short sleeves and deep, square neckline displayed the perfection of her beautiful skin.

"I believe Phoebe intends to play 'Jamie Douglas,'" Clive announced. When she nodded, he went on, "I apologize for being partial to such a lugubrious song, especially since this is such a festive occasion."

The guests found chairs or stood around the perimeter of the room. Edward went into the hall and returned with a chair, standing behind Deirdre after she sat down. As Phoebe began to play, words from the plaintive ballad ran through Deirdre's mind:

> *O fare thee well, my once lovely maid!*
> *O fare thee well, once dear to me!*
> *O fare thee well, my once lovely maid!*
> *For with me again ye shall never be.*

Deirdre sighed as she listened to the song telling of a wife abandoned by her husband. What, she wondered, had the unfortunate woman done to draw down such a punishment on her head?

Edward leaned over the back of her chair. "In Canada," he murmured, "I saw men who looked like that, men who had the same distracted look that Clive has. There may be more amiss with the man than we realize. Notice how attentive the good Dr. Leicester is."

The doctor, she saw, stood, his arms folded, a short distance from Clive. Though he appeared relaxed, his eyes never left Clive's face. Clive, who stood slightly behind Phoebe, stared straight ahead rather than watching her play. Phoebe, for her part, glanced down at the keyboard, looked up at her audience, but never looked at Clive, and in fact seemed to go out of her way to avoid looking at him.

Suddenly Clive took an uncertain, lurching step

forward. He reached for the top of the pianoforte, his hand sliding along the polished surface as he sought to gain his balance. Phoebe gasped, her hands dropping to the keyboard in a crashing discord. Deirdre half rose from her chair. Dr. Leicester strode to Clive's side at once, taking his arm and helping him to the couch, where Clive sat with his head buried in his hands.

The doctor murmured a few words to Clive and, when he failed to answer, took a candle, lit it, and, forcing Clive to look at him, passed it slowly back and forth in front of Clive's eyes.

Deirdre, thoroughly alarmed, turned to Edward. "What happened to him?" she asked.

"It may be his wound," he told her. "He could be reliving an unpleasant battle experience. All this hullabaloo may have brought it on."

The doctor, keeping his hand on Clive's shoulder, stood to face the guests. "Our friend is not in mortal danger," he told them in reassuring tones, "but he requires rest and quiet. I therefore intend to accompany him to his home without delay."

With one arm supporting Clive, the doctor led him from the room. Sybil came to Phoebe, who had half risen from the piano bench, and whispered a few words in her ear. After a moment's hesitation, Phoebe nodded and followed the two men from the room.

Roger Darrington raised his hand. "I consider it best," he said, "that we conclude the festivities now." He was answered by a murmur of assent. "When Clive has recovered," Roger added, "all of you are hereby invited to be my guests once more."

Phoebe returned home within the hour but ate dinner in her chamber rather than joining the family. Sybil, though, brought word from her daughter that Clive was now resting comfortably. Dr. Leicester, she reported, anticipated a full recovery.

Despite this comforting news, when Deirdre retired for the night, she discovered she could not sleep. After an hour of fretful tossing, she put on her robe and went down the shadowed stairs, intending to fetch a book from the library with the hope, though not the expectation, that she could read herself to sleep.

As Deirdre approached the partly open door of the library, she was surprised to see a single candle burning on one of the tables inside the room. Pausing in the doorway, she heard muffled sobs, and when she looked into the glass over the mantel, she saw the reflection of Phoebe, sitting huddled on the seat of a high-backed chair.

About to back away quietly and return undetected to her room, she stopped when Phoebe glanced up at the mirror, gave a start of recognition, and began dabbing at her face with a lace-edged handkerchief.

"I assure you, there is nothing—" Phoebe began, only to have tears again course down her cheeks.

Deirdre hurried to her, kneeling at her side, murmuring words of comfort.

"You must despise me," Phoebe said. "All of you."

Deirdre, confused, shook her head. Why should she despise Phoebe?

"For the unseemly way I behaved toward Clive today," Phoebe explained. "When I should have offered him words of comfort, I turned my face away. When I should have tried to help him, I thought only of myself. Can I help being the way God made me?" she asked plaintively. "Can you? Can any of us?"

"The long days of anticipation," Deirdre said softly, "the excitement of seeing him at last, followed by the shock of his having been wounded, over-whelmed you. Time will heal his wound."

"What of mine?" Phoebe shook her head dolefully. "Will my wound heal? What am I to do about Clive, about our betrothal? What would you do if you were in my place, Deirdre?"

"Why, marry Clive just as though nothing had happened. He is, despite his wound, the same man we said goodbye to months ago."

"Yes, I expect you would marry him, Deirdre. How like you to make the noble gesture and then wait to hear everyone applaud your unselfish devotion . . . even while you realize the marriage might be the greatest mistake of your life."

Deirdre barely controlled her anger. How waspish Phoebe could be, always ready to retaliate by stinging others with her sharp tongue after she herself had been hurt. "I fail to understand," she said, "how you could consider marrying Clive a great mistake."

"Because Clive has changed. How can you say this is the same man I bade farewell to before he sailed off to war? Surely you must have seen how peculiarly he behaved at the party today . . . like a total stranger. Could you bring yourself to marry a stranger?"

"I believe the change in Clive is only on the surface. With a little time and the thoughtful affection of all of his friends — "

"Time! You constantly speak of time, Deirdre, of months, of years. I celebrated my nineteenth birthday on the thirteenth of last May!" She glanced up at the looking glass. "See the shadows under my eyes, the

73

lines at their corners?"

Deirdre fought down her impatience. Phoebe's eyes might be shadowed from crying, but her beauty was undiminished. Her anguish seemed real, even though misplaced. Phoebe thought of herself first and foremost.

"Everyone speaks of your beauty," Deirdre assured her. "All the women at the Harmon ball, as well as Clive, James Aldrich, Edward — everyone."

"Edward?" Phoebe asked with quickening interest. "He has?"

Had he? Deirdre searched her memory without success. "His many admiring glances in your direction speak for him," she said.

"Edward has been most attentive," Phoebe said. As she dried her tears and then tucked her handkerchief beneath the belt of her blue robe, Deirdre rose from the floor and sat in a chair next to her.

"I was told by a little bird," Phoebe said, "that you and Edward were observed earlier today flying a kite in the park."

Deirdre smiled at the memory. "We did fly a kite, a gift from Edward intended for his young nephew. A kite he fashioned himself."

"Clive has told me time and again," Phoebe said, "that he has always thought of you as a little sister. And now, evidently, Edward has come to share his feelings, treating you like the younger sister he never had."

Annoyed and hurt, even though she had had much the same feeling herself, Deirdre wanted to say, "At least, being only eighteen rather than twenty, I have a few more years before I must face the hideous prospect of spinsterhood." The cruelty of the words persuaded her to hold her tongue, however, and she said nothing in reply to Phoebe's barb.

"Edward, of course," Phoebe said, "means absolutely nothing to me." She looked directly at Deirdre, her blue eyes still glistening with tears. "I love Clive," she said, almost defiantly, "with all my heart. Since I only want him to be happy, I fear a precipitous marriage could make both of us miserable for the rest of our days."

After a few moments' thought, Deirdre said, "Rather than marrying Clive at once, you might consider waiting a few months, perhaps have a Christmas wedding."

"The boughs of fir over the mantel, the holly, the mistletoe." Phoebe closed her eyes as though picturing the scene. "My wedding gown a pristine white silk, as white as the frost on the windowpanes, as white as the snow falling gently outside." She opened her eyes. "Yes, a postponement until Christmas is the very thing, and you, Deirdre, are a dear for suggesting it."

Standing, she took Deirdre's hand, and together they left the library.


Two days later, Deirdre was in the drawing room, working on her embroidery, when Alcida burst into room.

"Phoebe and Clive have agreed to delay their wedding," Alcida cried. "Phoebe just this minute told me. 'To allow time for the two of us to become reacquainted after Clive's dreadful experience,' she said."

Deirdre, not surprised, nodded. "Postponed until Christmas?"

"Christmas?" Alcida shook her head. "Phoebe made no mention of settling on a new date. In fact, she said the delay was quite indefinite, the length depending, I imagine, on Clive's regaining his health." She lowered her voice to a conspiratorial whisper. "Vincent believes his affliction is more of the mind than of the body, a condition he has observed in many men returning from the war."

So he was Vincent now, Deirdre thought fleetingly, rather than Dr. Leicester. "If only I could find a way to help Clive," Deirdre said fervently, without stopping to consider her words.

Alcida glanced sharply at her, but only said, "Everyone who knows Clive shares your feelings. Phoebe, I expect, more than any of us. Yet, how can we help when, as Vincent has told me, he spurns all assistance, absolutely refusing to speak of his experiences in Spain?"

On the following Monday, Dr. Leicester drew Deirdre to one side and repeated what he had told Alcida. "You knew Clive when he was young," the doctor went on, "and he often speaks fondly of your rides and rambles in East Sussex. In fact, he seems to consider you to be almost a member of his family. I believe his condition might be improved by a return — in his mind, at least — to the carefree days of his boyhood. Since you were often with him during those happier days, perhaps you can help Clive."

"If only I could."

"Will you come with me to see him?"

"Of course," she told him. "When?"

"I rather think it should be now."

# Chapter Seven

"Clive has taken lodgings in Bloomsbury," Dr. Leicester told Deirdre as they drove along Oxford Street. Noting her surprise, he added, "He thought it best to live apart from everyone, even from his father, for a time. I attempted to dissuade him, but to no avail."

Deirdre, picturing Clive brooding alone in his bachelor lodgings, clasped her hands in distress. "How is he? Pray tell me the truth, Doctor."

"His wound, as you saw, has healed, which is remarkable, considering its severity, and his general physical condition is good, if not excellent." He shook his head. "The temper of his mind is something else again, and despite what most of my colleagues maintain, I believe the state of one's mind is just as important as the condition of one's body—perhaps even more important.

"An American, Dr. Benjamin Rush, did considerable research on the subject during the revolt of the Colonies, and discovered that events occurring in the war could affect the human body through the medium of the mind. He stated, and I hope I quote him accurately, that 'the reciprocal influence of the body and mind upon each other can only be ascertained by an accurate knowledge of the faculties of the mind.' Which knowledge, alas, we do not have."

"I would think," Deirdre said, "a physical ailment caused by the mind would be most difficult to cure."

Dr. Leicester nodded. "Precisely. Let me give you but one example: despite having been a cavalry officer, he now absolutely refuses to mount a horse. At the same time, he gives no reason for his reluctance. Despite all my entreaties, Clive absolutely refuses to discuss whatever it is that troubles him. I hoped that you, a dear friend from his childhood, an amiable young woman, might be able to induce him to reveal, at least in part, whatever it is that is causing his unsettled state. I suspect that only when he confronts this hobgoblin will he be on the road to vanquishing it."

"What of Phoebe? She *is* his betrothed." Despite her best intentions, Deirdre felt a certain satisfaction that the doctor believed Clive might confide in her rather than in Phoebe.

"Phoebe has tried to induce him to speak, but to no avail." The doctor sighed. "You must be aware by now that their marriage has been put off indefinitely." When she nodded, he went on, "Clive seems to accept the delay, even gives evidence of being relieved by the postponement."

"Oh?" How surprising, she thought, if true. It well might not be, she ruefully told herself as she recalled the many times she had misread Clive's words or actions. Now Dr. Leicester may have done the same. Or was it possible that Clive's affection for Phoebe ran less deep than she or anyone else had imagined?

The doctor glanced at her, and when he spoke she could almost believe he had been reading her thoughts. "Clive insists he wants to marry Phoebe," he said, "and I have no reason to doubt him. I suspect he might—but enough of my speculations, let Clive speak for himself, if he happens to be so inclined. I can only conjecture; he knows his own heart and mind infinitely better than I do."

Deirdre wondered if, in fact, he did, after having to endure the last few tumultuous months. The heat of battle must be enough to temporarily cloud any man's mind. And when it came down to it, did anyone truly know his or her own mind? I do, she assured herself. Or at least, I know my own heart.

They found Clive waiting for them in a small garden, enclosed by a privet hedge, at the rear of his lodgings. The doctor, promising to return within the hour, left them seated side-by-side on a rustic pine bench at the far end of the rose arbor. To Deirdre, Clive appeared much as he had at the welcoming home party, seemingly calm, somber, and curiously lifeless.

"How young and alive you look," Clive said, nodding at her muslin afternoon gown. "Green becomes you, Deirdre." He shook his head sadly. "Your gown reminds me of the forest in East Sussex. Ashdown Forest. It brings to mind the glen, our glen, the good times we had there. All that seems so long ago. Years and years ago."

His speech, once so fluent, now seemed strangely disjointed. Despite her concern, Deirdre managed to smile. "Yet we last visited the glen only a few months ago," she reminded him.

79

He blinked, then nodded. "Of course, I remember," he said. "I carried the picture with me all the time I was in Spain."

Now it was her turn to be confused. "The picture?"

"Your portrait. I have it still, though I must admit I allowed it to become somewhat tattered and torn." He reached into an inside pocket of his waistcoat and brought forth a creased piece of drawing paper. Unfolding the paper with care, he smoothed it on his knee.

"Ah," she said, touched, "I remember now, the picture Mr. Turner drew after we came upon him sketching beside the bridge. How flattered I am you kept it all this time." *Just as I pressed and saved the wild rose you gave me that day,* she wanted to add, but dared not.

"I often looked at your likeness while in Spain," he said, "to remind me of home."

Clive carefully refolded her picture and replaced it in his pocket. Rising, he walked slowly to a nearby climbing rosebush, shaking his head as though his thoughts were elsewhere. He snapped off a half-opened white bud and cupped the flower in the palm of his hand as he stared down at it, frowning.

*He remembers his gift of the wild rose,* Deirdre told herself as tears misted her eyes, *and now he intends to give me another.*

Clive turned to her and, to her dismay, allowed the rosebud to slip from his hand to the ground. Looking over her head into the distance, he said, "Lord Wellington despised the cavalry. The cavalry gallops at anything and everything without preserving order, he claimed. The hussars never think of maneuvering when facing the enemy, he said. They never hold back or keep a reserve, he said. God knows, the cavalry would better serve me if they turned loose their horses and became infantry, he said."

Deirdre stared at him in amazement, not knowing what to make of his bitter comments. Could Wellington's poor opinion of the cavalry be what troubled Clive? she wondered. It seemed highly unlikely.

Clive put his hand to his wound, touching the scar lightly. "The terrible truth was this: Lord Wellington was right. He was absolutely right. In my first action—" He grimaced. "As it happened, it was also my last action. In my first action, our hussars charged the French, their swords unsheathed, with great gallantry. A magnificent spectacle, you never saw the like. But to no purpose, none at all."

Clive abruptly went to her and sat beside her on the bench. "Deirdre," he said, "do you swear to reveal nothing of what I am about to say? Do you swear a solemn oath?"

"Of course," she promised, her heart leaping with hope.

"To no one, not to Vincent, not even to Phoebe. Not now, not ever."

"I swear."

Clive nodded. "At times," he said, massaging his temple, "I become lightheaded. I hear the French cannon, or imagine I do." He blinked, looking away from her, toward the climbing roses. "Vincent claims the condition will subside with the passage of time. I have no reason to doubt him."

"While you were gone," Deirdre said, "I dreamed you were hurt in battle. The dream was so real that when I awoke I felt your pain."

He turned to her. "How strange. I seem to recall, though, my father once telling me your grandmother had the gift of being able to see into the future. Could you have inherited her ability?"

"I consider it a disability, as does Grandmama. She claims her dreams were a curse because, even though they were often right, just as often, they were so jumbled and confused they led her astray." Recalling her vision of Clive's wedding day, she wondered, as she had so many times before, what that dream meant.

"If only what happened to me were a dream and nothing more." Clive drew in his breath, pausing, his gaze fixed not on her, but inward, on a scene only he could see. When he spoke again, his words came in a rush. "We charged the French infantry. They scattered. We swept on, to their rear. To my left, some of our horses and riders plunged into a ravine. I saw the flash of French cannon firing from a wooded hill. We galloped up the hill." He shook his head and stopped.

"You need not go on," Deirdre told him.

He ignored her words. She wondered if he had even heard them.

"We charged up the hill. One of my men, Timmons, a young lieutenant, was unhorsed. I rode toward him. Intended to pull him onto the horse with me. I saw a flash of light. Heard a great roar."

When he again paused, she said very softly, so as not to break the spell of his remembering, "And then?"

Clive shook his head. "Nothing. I recall nothing at all, until I regained consciousness many hours later. By then it was night, and the French Army, thank

God, was in full retreat from the field of battle. The surgeon told me they found me not on the hill where I was wounded, but more than a half mile away. A half mile nearer our own infantry position."

He sounded so despondent, her heart went out to him. She reached to touch him on the arm, but drew back her hand at the last moment. "You remember nothing of what happened after you were wounded?" she asked encouragingly.

"Nothing. At least twelve hours have disappeared from my life. But there is one important circumstance I omitted from my account. And that exception is what haunted me then and haunts me now more than ever. Before I was wounded, I was afraid. Afraid, Deirdre. I never expected to be afraid."

"Everyone must fear for his life in battle," she protested, "even the heroic Lord Wellington. I imagine even Admiral Nelson often feared for his life."

"It was more than the fearing for my life," he said. "What troubles me most is that I have no memory of what I did after I was injured. I was found a half mile distant and closer to our own troops. Did I turn tail and flee the French? Was I a coward who deserted not only Lieutenant Timmons, but all my men?"

"You were wounded," she reminded him. "Seriously wounded. You must have been in a daze, probably unaware even of where you were or what you were doing. How can you possibly blame yourself for whatever happened?"

"An officer never deserts his men."

Deirdre, realizing he was determined to blame himself, decided to take another tack. "This Lieutenant Timmons—what did he say afterward?"

Clive shook his head. "Timmons either died of his wounds or was taken prisoner by the French, probably the latter, since his body was never found." Clive gripped her shoulder, making her wince. "Was I a coward, Deirdre? Did I desert my men? I have to learn the truth. Ah, if only you could help me."

If only she could, Deirdre told herself. But how could she? How?

"Vincent believes your visit raised Clive's spirits," Alcida said the following day, as they sat sewing in the morning room, "although Clive still refuses to discuss his affliction."

Remembering her promise to Clive to reveal nothing of the cause of his torment, Deirdre merely said, "I only hope he recovers completely as the weeks go by. I want to help him, but I have no notion how to go about it."

Deirdre laid aside her embroidery, a linen runner depicting red and green footmen holding aloft elaborate candelabras. Ever afterward, when she happened to look at her finished handiwork, she recalled these terrible, troubled days during which she so dangerously misconstrued the motives of others, of Phoebe, Clive, and Edward, while at the same time also failing to understand her own.

Alcida patiently rethreaded her needle. "Edward was here yesterday," she said, "supposedly to extend a dinner invitation to my mother and your father, but actually"—she glanced around and lowered her voice—"I do believe he came first and foremost to see Phoebe. She was all aflutter after he left."

"I fear Phoebe encourages him," Deirdre said. "Probably without meaning to."

"She does, without a doubt, and, moreover, to my mind deliberately. Though she *is* my sister, I must admit that Phoebe has always been a flirt. What I fear is that Edward is the sort of gentleman, and I used the word loosely, who wishes to reap some of what he considers to be the rewards of marriage without ever submitting himself to the wedding ceremony."

Deirdre, shocked, glanced sharply at Alcida. "Where did you come by such an idea?" she asked.

Alcida lowered her voice. "Do you promise to say nothing to Mama?"

"I promise," Deirdre assured her.

"The notion springs not from anything I am aware that Edward has actually done or attempted to do, although his reputation is not of the best, but from the monstrous actions of the villain in *The Secret Crypt of Octavio,* the novel I finished late last night. The heroine becomes entombed in Octavio's family burial vault and escapes Octavio's unwanted attentions only when she, quite by chance, turns the head of the griffin and thus opens the secret door to the passageway leading to the house. I often notice striking similarities between the characters in novels and the people I meet . . . as though the book was a mirror reflecting life."

Deirdre shook her head. "The novels I read invariably have the happiest of endings, while life often disappoints with either a tragic conclusion or no real conclusion at all."

"If we fail to stop Phoebe from pursuing this flirtation with Edward," Alcida said, "her story will certainly have an unhappy ending. And Clive's as well."

"And what precisely do you suggest?"

"That you strongly encourage Edward's attentions."

Deirdre stared at her. "Do you seriously think I should — ?"

"Hear me out. I think you must agree that Phoebe is in love with Clive, otherwise she would never have consented to marry him. Now, however, she has more than a few doubts both because of Clive's wound, which will result in a terrible scar" — Alcida slid her hand over her own pockmarked face — "and also because he behaves so strangely, so unlike the man she agreed to marry. Do you agree?"

Deirdre nodded.

"Clive is in love with Phoebe," Alcida went on, "otherwise he would never have asked her to marry him. Since his return to England, though, he has a great many doubts of his own, for reasons as yet unclear. Vincent — Dr. Leicester — expects him to recover, to become much the same person he was before he suffered his injury. So what we must do is give the two lovers an opportunity to become acquainted again. The main obstacle appears to be Edward. To my way of thinking, my sister believes Edward has feelings of tenderness for her."

"And yet, as you see it, he has no intention of ever marrying Phoebe."

"No, not Phoebe, not anyone. Edward is a rake comparable to the evil Mr. Lovelace in *Clarissa*. If you recall, after ravishing the heroine, he was killed in a duel with his best friend."

Deirdre, remembering her time with Edward in the

park, was about to demur, since he certainly had not played the rake with her. Yet she had to admit she hardly knew him. And, as Alcida and others had told her, his reputation suggested he was considerably less than a paragon.

"Therefore," Alcida said, "someone must distract Edward to give Phoebe the opportunity to accept Clive for a second time. Edward has, of course, scant interest in me. In any case, I have never acquired the knack of attracting a man. That leaves you, Deirdre, especially as both Vincent and I have noted the attention he pays you. When Phoebe played 'Jamie Douglas,' we both became aware of Edward watching you, not my sister."

Deirdre shook her head, both to spurn Alcida's suggestion and in disbelief at her notion that Edward had shown an interest in her. "What you suggest is quite impossible," she said. "I am not an accomplished flirt, and even if I were, I could never bring myself to flirt with Edward."

"Oh, but you have to try. Surely you could never forgive yourself if you consigned Phoebe to the sad fate of becoming the innocent prey to Edward's wicked advances, being first disgraced and then cast aside, causing Clive to die of a broken heart. Which is very nearly what happened to the two lovers in *The Turquoise Tower of Broadanger Belfry*."

"A most unlikely occurrence," Deirdre protested.

"Perhaps, yet do you have a better plan?" Alcida slanted a sideways glance at Deirdre. "Since, I believe, you do wish to do all in your power to help Clive."

"Of course I do!" Making up her mind in a rush,

Deirdre said, "It might succeed; your notion just might help Clive."

Alcida nodded vigorously. "And there can be no better occasion for putting our scheme to the test than Lord Harmon's alfresco party."

"An alfresco party? At Edward's father's country house?" It was the first Deirdre had heard of it.

"Every year we attend an October picnic and go nutting on the grounds of Lord Harmon's house on the banks of the Thames. While the rest of us are engrossed in gathering walnuts, you and Edward, I hope, will be engaged in quite a different diversion."

# Chapter Eight

Deirdre, alone in the chill of the night, hearing the seductive rise and fall of the music, pressed her face against the cold window glass to watch the fashionably dressed dancers inside the chandelier-lit ballroom come together, clasping hands above their heads, then part only to come together once more.

Clive danced with Phoebe, Clive handsome and unscarred, Phoebe beautiful in a pale blue gown, her blond ringlets framing her lovely, smiling face. Suddenly Clive glanced at the window and, although he gave no sign, Deirdre could tell he had seen her face there.

The dance ended. As Deirdre turned away into the night, the door to the ballroom opened and Clive stepped out onto the terrace and peered into the surrounding darkness. "Deirdre!" he called.

At first she hesitated, but then she stepped from the shadows into the oblong of light on the terrace. Clive smiled, holding his hand to her, urging her to come to him, and, after a brief moment of indecision, she started forward.

"No!" The man's voice came from behind her.

*Deirdre swung around to see Edward standing at the edge of the terrace, a long-barreled pistol in his hand. Clive strode toward him. She screamed and ran toward the two men, intending to fling herself between them, only to see the pistol flash and hear its ear-shattering roar.*

*Clive staggered backward, one hand clutching his forehead. Blood oozed from between his fingers. Murmuring her name, he seemed to recover, reaching toward her only to pitch forward onto the stones, where he lay unmoving. A sob burst from Deirdre's throat.*

*Edward calmly paused to reload his pistol, then aimed it across Clive's fallen body . . . at her. He meant to kill her, she realized. For a moment she stood facing him, frozen, and then, with a cry of terror, she turned and ran, ran down the stone steps, impeded by her skirt, ran across the dew-damp grass, smelling the sweet scent of the roses, all the while hearing Edward pursuing her, his footsteps coming closer and closer . . .*

*She glanced over her shoulder and saw his dark form silhouetted against the light from the ballroom. Her foot caught and she sprawled on her hands and knees on the grass. Rolling over onto her back, she looked up to see the half moon scudding between dark clouds. Edward loomed over her, moonlight glinting from the silver barrel of his pistol. The only sounds she heard were the rasp of her own breathing and the terrified pounding of her heart.*

*Edward knelt at her side, his actions slow and deliberate, and as she shrank away from him, he leaned to her, gripped her by the shoulders, and . . .*

90

* * *

Deirdre woke with a start and sat up in bed, her entire body trembling from the terror of the dream. It was only an ordinary dream, not a foreseeing one, she consoled herself. Not a vision, only a meaningless although terrifying dream.

She looked around her and saw the pale rectangle of the window, telling her it was almost morning. Today they would drive to Harmon Hall, Lord Harmon's country house, and tomorrow she would picnic along the Thames. With Edward. She shuddered, but almost immediately shook her head to dispel her fears. She had naught to fear from Edward, he meant her no harm, she assured herself; her dream signified nothing, nothing at all . . .

As Deirdre, Phoebe, Alcida, and Deirdre's father and stepmother left the Darrington townhouse in the chill of an October morning to start their journey, Deirdre became aware of an elderly couple — evidently residents of the neighborhood, since she had occasionally seen them strolling in the park — walking along the opposite side of the street.

In the past, they had taken no notice of her. Today they stared. Not at the Darrington party, not at Phoebe (strangers, struck by her beauty, were wont to stare at Phoebe), but at her. As Deirdre watched, the woman turned to her companion and spoke in a low voice. He nodded in vigorous agreement.

"Are they acquaintances of yours?" Alcida asked, her curiosity evidently piqued.

"They are not," Deirdre told her. "In fact, I have never spoken so much as a word to either of them."

"How rudely they look at you," Phoebe said. "They have the same gaping stares as children seeing an elephant in the menagerie for the first time. And they must be approaching their allotted three score and ten at the very least."

"Girls, we must be on our way," called Sybil, who was already seated in the traveling chaise.

"That elderly gentleman," Phoebe said, "gives every indication of wanting to cross the street and—" At a loss for what she expected him to do, she paused and added, somewhat lamely, "and I know not what. Does he intend to question you? To sing your praises?"

"Since I have never met him," Deirdre said, "I intend to ignore him."

Entering the chaise, she sat across from her father. After a few moments she heard the coachman's whip crack and they started forward, rattling over the cobbles on their way to Harmon Hall. Before they turned into Oxford Street, Deirdre glanced behind her and saw the couple staring after their carriage . . . after her, she was certain.

How strange, she thought, feeling both puzzled and vaguely upset. Was it possible, she wondered, that they had mistaken her for someone else? Perhaps she reminded them of an old friend. However, after their carriage stopped to pay the toll at the Edgeware Road turnpike and they left London behind, she forgot about the incident.

Her father, looking from the window at the overcast sky, shook his head. "Lord Harmon may well be forced either to forgo or postpone his picnic this year," he said.

"For five consecutive years," Sybil told Deirdre, "the weather has been quite delightful during the week Phoebe, Alcida, and I spent at Lord Harmon's." She shook her head. "This year, I fear the worst."

Deirdre noticed that a herd of cows in a pasture beside the road had clustered together with their heads facing away from the wind. "A sure sign of rain within twenty-four hours," her grandmother had often warned her.

"If rain comes, we shall have our picnic indoors," Phoebe said. "In fact I prefer the indoors, particularly at Harmon Hall, with its many amenities. Did you know that as a nation becomes civilized, its people tend to center their lives indoors rather than out?"

"She must have read that in a book," Alcida whispered to Deirdre.

"I heard what you said, Alcida," Phoebe told her, "and it was not from a book, it happens to be my own observation. It came to mind because only last week Edward told me of some of his fascinating experiences living with the Iroquois Indian tribe, describing how they hunt and fish in the wilderness. The Indians are certainly a primitive people while we, who spend most of our time indoors, are most assuredly civilized."

"And you, Deirdre," Alcida asked. "Which do you prefer?"

"The out-of-doors, without a doubt!" she said with a vehemence that surprised her. As Alcida and Phoebe chattered on, she settled back and closed her eyes, recalling her rides with Clive across the heath,

93

their many rambles in Ashdown Forest.

"— Clive —"

Phoebe's mention of Clive startled her from her reverie.

"He expects to accompany Dr. Leicester to Harmon Hall," Phoebe went on. "They hope to arrive tomorrow in time for the picnic."

"I observe little change in young Chadbourne," Roger Darrington said. "I hope and pray he recovers soon."

"The country air," Sybil said, "cannot help but have a salubrious effect on whatever it is that ails him."

"I greatly fear that he requires more than a breeze off the Thames to cure him." Roger shook his head sadly. "But what it is he does require, I have no notion, none at all."

At the first mention of Clive's malaise, Phoebe turned her head away to stare from the carriage window. Only when the subject lapsed did she turn to Deirdre. "The Harmon estate is nothing short of magnificent," she said. "The cost must have been enormous."

"One of England's great country houses," Roger said. "Dr. Johnson and his Boswell are only two of the many visitors who began journeying there almost from the day it was completed."

"And in time," Phoebe said, with what Deirdre took to be a wistful tone, "all of Harmon Hall will belong to Edward, the only son and heir."

Alcida glanced at Deirdre, her raised eyebrows clearly saying, "You can see what interests my sister. If you care for Clive and his happiness, you must discover a way to discourage her interest in Edward."

They passed through the gates to Harmon Hall in mid-afternoon and drove along a curving avenue, past a water wagon laying the dust. As they crossed a stone bridge whose three arches gracefully spanned a manmade lake, Deirdre was surprised to see, to her right and so near the lake that it was reflected in the placid waters, the white marble columns of a domed Grecian temple. For some unexplained reason, Deirdre felt a shiver of apprehension raise gooseflesh on her arms.

"The Harmon Pantheon," Phoebe said.

Once beyond the bridge, they entered a grove of ancient oaks and, when they came from under the trees, Deirdre gasped as she saw, across a wide expanse of open parkland and lawn, the magnificent house, a building in the style of classical Greece with a matched pair of stone steps leading up to the splendor of a portico whose six columns supported a pediment on top of which stood the statues of three gods: Venus in the center, representing beauty and fertility, flanked by Ceres, goddess of the harvest, and Bacchus, the god of wine.

The exterior of Harmon Hall was magnificent, awesome, and, Deirdre thought, rather overwhelming; when Edward led their party through the house, she found the interior, considered the greatest of Robert Adam's many achievements, built on a grand scale, with exquisite taste, yet more of a museum than a family residence.

The centerpiece of the Harmon country house was the great marble hall, whose alabaster columns rose more than twenty-five feet above the floor; it was a room without the distraction of windows — almost the entire ceiling was given over to a skylight — a room with the busts of English kings and queens set in niches on all four walls.

On the east side of the marble hall the drawing room, music room, and library represented the arts of painting, music, and literature, while the dining room and the bedchamber reserved for visiting royalty were on the west side. Two semidetached wings were connected to the main part of the house by corridors, with the kitchen wing on one side and the family and guest wing on the other.

The chapel, greenhouse, stables, carriage house, and the pantheon, Edward told them, were all located nearby on the extensive grounds, shielded from the main house by trees. Other, smaller structures included the fishing house and the boathouse, both on the Thames, a half mile from the main house.

Harmon Hall took Deirdre's breath away. She had never imagined that such splendor existed, much less that she would be invited to stay at such a country house as a friend of the family. Even as her sense of awe began to recede, she realized how tempted Phoebe must be by the attentions of Edward, the man who would one day be master of this vast domain. The opportunity to be the mistress of Harmon Hall would tempt almost anyone.

Does it tempt *me?* Deirdre asked herself that night as she lay in an ornate fourposter bed in her mauve bedchamber. She had always considered herself to be but little interested in possessions, had always considered the character of a person to be infinitely more important than what he happened to own. No, she had not changed, she decided as she slipped into sleep; while she admired the house's beauty, she had not been swayed by the opulence of Harmon Hall.

In the morning, Deirdre was drawing on her long pink gloves when there came a tapping at the door and Alcida entered.

"I quite approve of your gown," Alcida said, "with one reservation."

Deirdre wore an afternoon dress of white lawn with puffed sleeves and a deep vee décolletage modified by a lace-edged pink silk insert. Embroidery decorated the pink silk band at the dress's hemline.

"And that is?" Deirdre asked.

Looking about her, Alcida saw Deirdre's sewing basket, rummaged inside, and brought forth a pair of scissors. Before Deirdre knew what she intended, Alcida began snipping at the stitches holding the pink silk insert at the neckline of her gown.

"What are you doing?" Deirdre demanded as she hastily drew away.

"I intend to do for you exactly what the innocent heroine of *The Rake's Reward* did for herself. I mean to change you from a demure young country miss into a sophisticated enchantress."

"And the removal of an insert will accomplish such a miraculous transformation?"

"It cannot fail to help."

Even as Deirdre shook her head, Alcida advanced on her, scissors in hand. "I must," she said, "for now your insert hangs askew." She cut the remaining stitches and held up the triangle of silk in triumph. "You look quite—quite daring."

As Deirdre turned to the looking glass, the resonant bong of a bell told them the time had come to gather in the drawing room. She stared unhappily at her revealing décolletage while Alcida tugged at her arm.

"Come," Alcida said, "we must leave for the picnic at once."

Deirdre reached for her pink silk paisley shawl, drawing it around her shoulders and covering the deep vee between her breasts. Unfortunately, she could hardly clutch the shawl in such an unbecoming manner without causing comment. Sighing, she draped it properly over her arms.

"Hurry," Alcida urged from the doorway.

Deirdre had imagined the picnic as a casual affair, had pictured a short stroll from the house to the parkland, where the picnickers would serve themselves to simple country fare from tablecloths spread on the grass.

Such was not the case. The guests left the house in ten carriages, drove through the park to the river, passing the fishing house — "Designed so that ladies," Edward explained to them, "may cast their lines for fish from the window overlooking the river, so they will not have to be exposed to the elements" — and stopping beside a grassy expanse near the boathouse where, earlier that morning, tables and chairs had been arranged in a great circle.

After being seated, they were served course after course, with offerings of venison, lamb, partridge, quail, pigeons, and carp, of Severn salmon and Dunstable larks, along with a variety of vegetables and followed by puddings and tarts, the meal accompanied by vintage Bordeaux wine imported from

France in the years before the war.

As she ate, Deirdre noticed that Edward, seated almost directly across the circle from her and so at too great a distance for polite conversation, glanced at her more than once, each time nodding and smiling. Resisting an impulse to draw her shawl over her décolletage, she wished with all her heart that she had never allowed Alcida to remove the silk insert.

When they had at last finished their meal, the large company was left free to follow their personal inclinations, whether rowing on the Thames, engaging in companionable discourse while seated on benches along the bank of the river, or, for the more adventuresome, archery on the lawn or nutting in the nearby walnut grove.

"Where can Vincent and Clive be?" Alcida asked as she and Deirdre, carrying their furled parasols, walked along a pathway beside the river. "They should have arrived by now. Can Clive have refused to come at the last moment?"

"He may have," Deirdre said, concealing both her unhappiness at the thought of not seeing him and her distress at his disturbed state of mind. "He may wish to avoid the confusion, the crush."

"Ah, look," Alcida said, clearly disappointed as she nodded toward several couples carrying baskets as they made their way toward the walnut grove. "Edward and Phoebe have decided to accompany the nutting excursion. Shall we tag along after them?"

Deirdre shook her head. The more she considered it, the more the notion of attempting to entice Edward away from Phoebe seemed the height of folly . . . as well as a quite hopeless undertaking. Edward must have the female portion of the *ton* virtually at his feet, and she had neither the desire nor the inclination to join them.

Pushing her hair back from her face, Alcida looked across the river at the darkly threatening sky. "I hope it rains and both Phoebe and Edward are thoroughly soaked."

Deirdre smiled at Alcida's outburst, but said nothing as she led the way along the path. When the boathouse was lost to sight behind them, they turned and retraced their steps, remarking now and again as a particularly pleasing river vista came into view.

When they reached the boathouse once more, Deirdre stopped beside the door and looked around her, unable to resist her impulse to search for Clive. He was nowhere to be seen. Noticing her father instructing Sybil in the intricacies of the bow and arrow, Deirdre said, "Shall we try our skill?"

The door to the boathouse suddenly opened and, as Deirdre gasped, Edward stepped onto the path a few feet in front of them. He looked at Deirdre; only at Deirdre. His lack of surprise at meeting her in this unexpected manner made her wonder if he had been waiting for her to return.

"Ever since I arrived at home at Harmon Hall from Canada," he said, finally acknowledging Alcida with a gracious bow, "I have been promising myself a row on the river. Will you two young ladies honor me with your company?"

Alcida ducked her head. "Thank you, my lord, but even the slightest motion of the water has a most unfortunate effect on me." She curtsied. "I must go to Mama," she said with a quick glance at Deirdre and, without another word, hurried off.

"I expect the rain to start at any moment," Deirdre told him.

"Damn the rain." He held out his hand to her. She hesitated. "Please," he said.

When still she hesitated, he reached to her and put his hand gently on her arm. "You must come with me," he said. "Say you will."

After all, she reminded herself, Edward was their host; she could hardly refuse him and thus create an awkward situation. And yet some inner voice warned her not to accept his offer, a reluctance, she chided herself, undoubtedly brought on by her foolish dream. Since she had quite convinced herself that she had nothing to fear from Edward, Deirdre quieted her trepidation and nodded.

## Chapter Nine

Edward rowed from the boathouse onto the Thames with Deirdre sitting in the stern, facing him. How delightful she looked in her white gown, he told himself, with her flaming red hair only partially hidden by her pink bonnet. Even though the day was overcast and rain threatened, she had unfurled her parasol and held it over her head to complete the picture.

"You make a charming picture," Edward told her. "Pray excuse my staring at you, but I must etch every detail on my memory to recall tomorrow when, unfortunately, I must join the other gentlemen in the east copse for the shooting."

Made uneasy by his compliment, Deirdre said nothing.

"I only hope," Edward said, "the poachers have left us a few quail and partridge."

"We have more than our share of poachers in Sussex," Deirdre said.

"At Harmon Hall, we refuse to set out man traps or spring guns to deter the intruders, so we are forced to depend on our gamekeepers . . . who may be poachers themselves." He smiled. "I happen to have a certain sympathy with poachers. After all, you can make a case that the fowl of the air and the deer and other animals that roam the forests belong to everyone."

Edward might well sympathize with poachers, Deirdre told herself. He was reputed to be one himself, although his prey was neither fowl nor deer.

As soon as they left the shallows and entered the river's strong current, Edward shipped the oars and allowed the boat to drift downstream. Reaching beneath his seat, he brought forth a red wooden box, pushed the latch free, and opened the lid to reveal a magnum of champagne and two long-stemmed glasses nestled in blue velvet.

"Champagne is truly a wine fit for a goddess," he said, as he inserted a corkscrew.

"I —" Deirdre began, but suspecting she meant to decline, Edward immediately held up his hand and shook his head.

"Would you disappoint me," he asked, "by refusing to join in celebrating my birthday?" The cork came free with an explosive *pop,* and he proceeded to fill the two glasses and hand one to her.

"This is your birthday?" she asked, as she accepted the glass.

"Since I happened to be on the high seas on the actual date of my birth, I intend to celebrate today." Raising his glass, he reached forward to touch its rim to hers, watching Deirdre as she leaned to him and, in so doing, revealed the tempting swell of her breasts.

Edward drew in a quick breath. Be patient, he

counseled himself, as he damped down his desire. She was so innocent, so lacking in experience; undoubtedly she was a virgin. And yet, or so he had suspected from the first, beneath her prim exterior there seethed a passion as fiery as her hair, a passion ready to erupt once the shackles of convention had been stripped away.

He smiled confidently. He, Edward Fox, Marquess of Lounsbury, sole heir to Harmon Hall, fully intended to be the one to free her from those restraints; he would be the one who would lead her to a discovery of the voluptuous world of the senses, a world he had thoroughly explored and thus knew as well as anyone.

And he intended to do it this very day.

A single-masted barge sailed past them, heading upriver, and one of the bargemen sitting near the stern waved his hand as he called to them across the water.

"He envies me," Edward told Deirdre.

Ignoring her reluctance to accept more of the champagne, Edward smiled encouragingly as he refilled her glass, noting the slight flush on her cheeks. "This is your first visit to Harmon Hall, I believe," he said.

"And my first taste of champagne; my grandmother refuses to have spirits of any kind in the house. The Hall is magnificent, actually there are no words to do it justice; and the wine is delicious."

"My ancestors first came here more than six hundred years ago," he told her, as he dipped the oars in the water and rowed downstream. "They were Normans who fought with William the Conqueror."

Proudly—he was exceedingly proud of his heritage—he described the ascent of the Foxes, their bitter rivalry with the Cavendish family of nearby Oakcroft, the expansion of the estate until it encompassed more than ten thousand lucrative acres of farmland, and the planning and building of Harmon Hall in the first half of the eighteenth century, first under the direction of James Paine, the architect, and then under the direction of the young Robert Adam.

"When I become master here," he said, aware that there were no greater aphrodisiacs than wealth and power, "and that, I pray to God, will not be for a great many years, I plan to carry on the family traditions. Did you happen to notice our motto, carved on the north front of the Hall?" When Deirdre shook her head, he said, "It reads, 'Amicis et sibi.' "

" 'For his friends and himself'?"

"Ah, wonderful, you know Latin. Precisely. And that is what Harmon Hall will always be as long as I live, a place of hospitality designed for the pleasure of Lord Harmon and his many friends. And, in due course," he added with just a touch of emphasis, "for the pleasure of the wife of Lord Harmon as well."

She blinked, frowning slightly. "At the ball, you claimed to have returned to England with absolutely no intention of marrying."

"Every man, including myself," he said, his gaze meeting hers in a meaningful way, "is entitled to reconsider his intentions as circumstances change." After a pause, he said, "I suggested rowing on the

Thames so I'd have the opportunity of showing you our pantheon. If you will but look over my right shoulder, you should see the white dome rising above the trees."

She did as he asked, saying, "The little I can see of the pantheon is most impressive. As for viewing the rest, perhaps another day, Edward, when the weather is less threatening. We should turn back at once."

"I give you my word, my dear Deirdre, there will be no rain to mar our excursion. I absolutely forbid rain to fall on my birthday. Or on someone as lovely as yourself."

In fact, he expected rain and had been surprised that the storm had not arrived sooner. Not that it mattered; whether it rained or not, he meant to escort her to the pantheon, but not merely to show her the splendor of the rotunda with its statues of Greek gods and goddesses. Again Edward smiled. Not even his father—who had sent him in great haste to Canada to avoid scandal—was aware of the secrets of the pantheon.

Some five years before, Edward had expressed an interest in painting, just as he had once dabbled in the writing of romantic poetry. His father had suggested he use an empty apartment in the pantheon for his studio, since the light from its northern exposure of one of the rooms was ideal, and Edward had agreed.

Though he had enjoyed working with watercolors—and, later, with oils—his enthusiasm had waned when he began to seek to satisfy the demands of the flesh rather than the spirit. He had completely redecorated his three private rooms in the pantheon, assisted in his purchases by a rather disreputable London dealer in certain European and Oriental works of literature and art of a sort sold primarily to gentlemen who had what were referred to as "special tastes." Edward had paid one of the Hall's stableboys, Jack Cunningham, and rather handsomely, to perform the necessary laboring work and thereafter to guard his secret by holding his tongue.

Smiling in anticipation, Edward dipped his oars deep in the murky depths of the Thames and stroked, and the boat shot ahead. He exulted in rowing as he did in sports of all kinds, in fencing, cricket, archery, and pugilism; enjoyed testing himself against others; savored his frequent victories while shrugging off his occasional defeats.

He considered the pursuit of women to be a sport worthy of a gentleman, a contest involving careful reconnaissance followed by pursuit requiring a knowledge of when to speak the truth and when to embroider it, when to flatter or cajole and when to command. Perhaps, he told himself, warfare was a better analogy than sport, since it was a battle requiring both deception and strength, the male attacking as the female executed a strategic retreat, the final triumph of the male followed by the subjection of the conquered by the conqueror.

Deirdre, he noted, had peeled off one of her gloves and was trailing her bare hand in the water. "How lovely you are," he said, quite sincerely, "Diana reincarnated. Your statue should be in our pantheon, a goddess among the other goddesses."

107

She stared at him in surprise as though recalling—what? Intuitively, he said, "Someone else has compared you to a goddess."

Could it have been Chadbourne? he wondered, suspecting, from hints dropped by Phoebe, that Deirdre and Clive had been rather close childhood friends. Could they have been lovers? He doubted it; no, if all went as well as he expected, he would be the first.

A charmingly vivid flush spread over her face. "A painter did once, a Mr. Joseph Turner."

"Turner?" he asked. When she nodded, he said, "Having once tried my hand at painting, although an amateur, I believe I have a certain knowledge of the art. I happen to be a great admirer of his work, and especially his sense of color, his vibrant landscapes. I can think of no better authority on feminine beauty than Turner."

Most men, Edward mused, would consider Phoebe to be a greater beauty than Deirdre; as usual, most men were mistaken. Phoebe might boast a pleasing regularity of feature, a fair complexion, lovely golden hair, and the sweet bloom of youth, but in a few years her beauty would begin to fade. Deirdre, on the other hand, possessed a classic beauty, a natural grace, a liveliness of spirit—and, best of all in his estimation, the promise of an underlying and as yet unleashed passion.

If the truth be told, he considered Phoebe to be rather insipid, a narcissist interested in no one but herself. Phoebe always succeeded in boring him with her self-absorption, while Deirdre fascinated him with her wealth of contradictions. Was she really the innocent she had at first seemed, to be or was she the temptress suggested by this daring décolletage? He meant to find the answer before many hours passed.

What had she just asked him? Whether he had built a new kite for Ned, yes, that was it. He searched his memory as he tried to recall exactly what he had told her about the kite. "I did indeed," he said, "and, furthermore, only last week I presented it to him and helped him launch it into the heavens."

"You were most kind to give the kite to the boy in the park," she said.

Edward sketched a bow to acknowledge the compliment. In truth, both kites — there had been two, and Ned had received one of them, that was true enough — had been the handiwork of Jack Cunningham, the same stableboy at Harmon Hall who shared the secret of his rooms in the pantheon. His gift of the kite to the urchin in the park had not been made so much to please the boy, but rather to impress Deirdre with his generosity. Edward congratulated himself on a minor, though obviously successful, ploy.

He scowled briefly, not because he felt any shame at his small deception — far from it, he rather admired his cleverness in having thought of asking her to fly the kite with him — but because he suddenly experienced a strange sense of loss . . . for the second time in recent days. When was the first? he wondered. Of course, in the park, when he had held the twine and watched the kite soar above the trees and then glanced at Deirdre, seeing her face aglow. For a moment he had imagined himself a boy again and had savored that time in his life when everything seemed possible.

A drop of rain striking his forehead brought him from his reverie. Again glancing at Deirdre, her parasol still raised, he realized she was unaware that the storm no longer merely threatened, but had arrived. Looking over his shoulder, he saw they were only a few hundred feet from the small dock and the path leading away from the river to the pantheon.

Soon, he promised himself, very soon. "You must finish your champagne," he said. "Once uncorked, the wine soon becomes flat."

After drinking the last of it, Deirdre put the glass aside, lowered and furled her parasol, and then raised her hands heavenward, as though to embrace the day. Suddenly she crossed her arms over her breasts and frowned. "I felt rain," she said. "We must turn about."

"We have come too far," he said, "to return in time to avoid a drenching. Look ahead of us, Deirdre, see the dock and the path. We can find shelter in the pantheon, and wait there until this shower passes over."

She started to protest, but when he dipped one oar deep into the water to swing the boat toward shore, she raised her parasol again and said nothing.

He asked himself, as he customarily did when he met an attractive and eligible young lady, what sort of wife this Deirdre Darrington would make. Even though he would one day become Lord Harmon of

110

Harmon Hall, he had no intention of marrying merely for wealth and position. Why should he, when he was already more than well-supplied with both? Nor would he marry only for that other reason often deemed a requisite for wedded bliss—particularly by females of the species—that overrated, indefinable something called love.

His marriage, when the time finally came, would be for one primary purpose: the siring of a son and heir. His father had produced three sons, but only he, Edward, had survived infancy. His wife must perforce be of sturdy stock and, from the look of her, Deirdre more than qualified. She would produce thoroughbreds.

Not that he completely eschewed romance. He would never make the grievous error committed by the Prince Regent and marry a woman he deemed to be ugly and unappealing. Good God, how ludicrous to select a future queen from sketches drawn by sycophantic artists! He, Edward, intended to marry someone who appealed to him in a romantic way.

There were many such women, and Deirdre was certainly one of them. He scoffed at those who claimed a man should love but one woman, a notion propagated, he supposed, by women of a literary bent. The idea was preposterous, completely absurd, and he suspected that even those who espoused it knew better than to believe or follow it.

Although Deirdre appealed to him, he had decided she would be unacceptable as a wife because he suspected she would be much too unconventional. The conventional wife of a gentleman of the *ton* quickly learned to ignore her husband's amorous adventures, his affairs, his succession of mistresses. The conventional wife might even take a lover of her own.

Deirdre, on the other hand, would be faithful to her spouse, which, of course, he considered an excellent trait in a woman, but she would also demand faithfulness in return, a notion that was completely repugnant and absolutely unacceptable to Edward and any other civilized gentleman in the Year of Our Lord 1813.

And so, albeit with more than a little regret, Edward had struck a line through the name of Miss Deirdre Darrington where it appeared on his mental list of possible mates. The challenge she would provide, the hoped-for, nay, the expected fire, the passion, would not be worth the aggravation of being forced to defend himself in the face of her harangues when she learned of what she would certainly consider his unfaithfulness.

When Edward felt the boat nudge against the dock, he shipped the oars, stood, and walked to the prow. He leaped to the dock as the rain fell harder, making tiny circles in the water below him. After tying the boat to a metal ring on the dock, he looked down to find that Deirdre had already stepped from the boat to the planking. Though she attempted to shelter herself under her parasol, rain was already seeping through the thin silk of her dress.

Offering her his arm, he waited until she reached out to take it and then grasped her hand. She had not replaced her glove, and her fingers were warm and soft in his. Almost at once she tugged her hand away, gave him a speaking look, and took his arm. Glancing at her as they started along the path leading up the bank and away from the river, he saw the upper curve of her breast and, for an instant, imagined his hand gently pushing aside her gown, imagined his fingers brushing over her nipple—

Feeling the rising pulse of excitement, he shook his head to dispel the image. He had been foolish to take her hand in his. He must, he warned himself, do nothing to alarm her, nothing to cause her to dart away from him like a frightened deer.

They came to the stile—"the fence is for the horses," he explained—and he climbed to the far side, helped her to the top, then reached up and grasped her about the waist and swung her to the ground, unable to resist the temptation to hold her for a fraction of a second longer than necessary, relishing the softness of her body beneath his fingers, breathing in the delicate scent of her, at the same time cursing his impulsiveness when he noted the glint of fright in her green eyes.

He longed to slide his hands around her body and urge her slowly into his embrace, wanted to bury his face in the sweet hollow of her neck while his fingers gently caressed her nape, to draw back and look down at her as her eyes closed and her lips parted in a silent invitation.

Soon, he assured himself . . . soon she will be more than willing to give you all that you long for.

As she again took his arm, this time more hesitantly, the rain swept across the meadow and the nearby lake, stinging his face and soaking his coat and trousers. A sidelong glance showed him that Deirdre's gown now clung wetly to the delightful curves of her body, from her breasts to her hips to her thighs.

Edward looked from Deirdre, with her fiery hair, to the pantheon, rising pure and white beside the roiled waters of the lake, to the clouds massing above the dome; struck by the beauty of the scene, he involuntarily drew in his breath.

His steps lagged. Was he making a great mistake? he asked himself. Was it possible that Deirdre was different, completely unlike any of the other young women in his life? Could it be that, married to Deirdre, he would want to remain faithful, would want to give up the life he had enjoyed for so long?

What manner of sorcery was at work? he wondered. What a fanciful notion, how surprising that it had entered his mind even for a moment. Deirdre might have the appearance of a goddess, but she would prove no different from all the others. Brushing his errant thought aside, he walked on more quickly than before.

The pantheon, the glory of its white marble partially obscured by the slanting rain, loomed in front of them. They hurried up the steps and through an archway into the domed rotunda where, he thought, the gods watched him jealously from their niches.

Without pausing, he led Deirdre from the rotunda into a hallway leading to a small anteroom. Here there were no statues; the carved heads of wolves, bears, and other beasts of the forest stared down from the walls, tokens of a more primitive time when men hunted in these forests and sacrificed to pagan deities. He noticed Deirdre looking askance at the beasts.

Edward reached into a crevice beside a massive door, his fingers closing on a large iron key. Inserting the key into the lock, he turned it, opened the door, and stood aside so she could see past him to the fire burning in the grate on the far side of the room.

"I have a surprise prepared for you," he said as he escorted her into the room, "a very pleasant surprise."

## *Chapter Ten*

She was doing this for Clive, Deirdre had told herself when she accepted Edward's invitation to accompany him in his rowboat on the Thames. She would force Phoebe to realize how inconstant Edward was, how short-lived and shallow his affections were, and thus encourage Phoebe to turn once more to Clive and give him the comfort and attention he so desperately needed.

From the very first, being alone in the small boat with Edward caused Deirdre a vague uneasiness. She found it impossible to dismiss from her mind her vivid dream of Edward shooting Clive outside the ballroom, of Edward threatening and then pursuing her. It *was* only a dream, she tried to assure herself, a figment of her much-too-active imagination. Her fears were baseless, for Edward meant Clive no harm; he meant her no harm.

Unable to quell her fears completely, she accepted Edward's offer of champagne, hoping the wine would help dull her misguided apprehension and permit her to savor what should be a very special moment. Despite the threat of rain, she should be admiring the splendid rural vistas along the river while enjoying the company of one of the most eligible gentlemen in all of England.

And the champagne did provide a soft glow, did allow her to relax enough to peel off one of her gloves and trail her hand in the water. Yet she was disquieted anew when Edward insisted on rowing to shore and taking her to the pantheon even after she called his attention to the darkening sky and suggested it would be better to return another time. It seemed to Deirdre that even before they left the boathouse he had decided on what they would do and nothing she said would sway him.

She disliked the way he looked at her as he rowed downstream, distrusted the glint in his eyes as he watched her. His was not a look of camaraderie or admiration, but a predatory stare that sent tiny shivers along her spine, not a pleasant, anticipatory tingle but one of apprehension, almost fear.

The scheme to entice Edward—how she disliked the word *entice*—Deirdre quickly decided, had been a horrendous mistake. She should never have allowed Alcida to persuade her against her better judgment. What she had intended to do was not only dishonest, and unfair to Edward; at the same time it ran counter to her nature.

When the rain began and Edward tied the boat at the dock and led her along the path to the pantheon, she accompanied him with great reluctance. She found him much too forward. Not that she considered his clasping her bare hand or his holding her about the waist as he helped her from the stile unduly alarming. Perhaps this was the way gentlemen of the *ton* behaved, but she did not care for such uninvited overfamiliarity.

Her trepidation increased, however, when he led her inside the darkened pantheon. As he unlocked the door to one of the inner chambers, she hesitantly placed her sopping parasol against the wall before reluctantly preceding him into the room where she was surprised to find a fire crackling in the grate.

"I have a surprise prepared for you," he said, "a very pleasant surprise."

Doing her best not to reveal her growing apprehension, she crossed the room to the fire, stepping around a large bearskin rug spread on the floor, and held out her hands to the warming flames.

"Before we left the Hall this morning," he told her, "I asked one of the stableboys to ride here to start the fire, in the event the day turned cold."

She had been right, Deirdre told herself — Edward had planned to come here from the first. "How wonderful the fire feels," she said, as she looked not at him but into the dancing flames.

"Here, pray allow me to give you this," he told her almost brusquely. When she turned to him, he was holding the key to the door. "For your peace of mind," he said, "take this key and lock the door behind me. I plan to leave at once to walk to the carriage house and return to fetch you in a rig."

Deirdre let her breath out in a quiet sigh of relief. Though not certain what she had expected him to do, it was not this eminently proper behavior. Perhaps she had misjudged him from the very beginning, or else the fault had been more hers than his. Her hand rose to cover the deep vee of her neckline.

"I may have something here to help you dry yourself," Edward said, crossing the room and opening the lowest drawer of a chest. When he returned he offered her a cloth and, while she wiped the water from her face, he pulled a covering from a table.

"A silk shawl for milady," Edward said, as he draped the covering over the back of one of the chairs. Bowing, he strode to the door only to pause and glance back at her. "The carriage house," he told her, "is almost three miles from here, and so I shall be absent for at least an hour." He left the room, closing the door behind him, and she heard his footsteps recede.

Deirdre locked the single door, careful to leave the key in the lock. As she returned to the hearth, she glanced warily about the room. Since there were no windows, the only light came from the fire, the flickering flames throwing grotesque shadows on the dark-red walls; surprisingly, she saw no candles or lamps on any of the tables.

There were, she noticed, a large number of oil paintings on two of the walls, but in the uncertain flickering light from the fire she was unable to see them clearly. The other two walls contained tier upon tier of glass-fronted bookcases extending from the floor to the ceiling. Though she knew not why, the room made her uneasy, giving her an eerie feeling that she was not alone, but in the presence of a watching, brooding evil.

How morbidly fanciful you are, Deirdre told herself. This is merely a room—a man's room, perhaps, but nothing more. Any uneasiness you feel comes from wanting to be elsewhere.

She untied and removed her wet bonnet and hung

119

it from a hook at one end of the mantel. Her damp and bedraggled hair, she realized, was absolutely beyond salvation. Her dress clung soddenly, chillingly, to her body, causing her to shiver and clasp her arms across her breasts. Despite the warmth of the fire, the muslin seemed to resist drying.

Again Deirdre glanced warily around the shadowed room. She saw nothing. She breathed in, thinking she had caught a whiff of some strange and pungent odor reminiscent of incense. One of the logs in the fireplace crackled and, as sparks scattered on the grate, she decided the scent must come from the burning wood.

Standing in front of the fire, she shook her head at her ridiculous fears as she welcomed the warmth suffusing her face and hands even as she shivered from the chill of her wet clothing on the rest of her body. With a sigh, she closed her eyes, suddenly exhausted, the heat and the wine combining to induce a pleasant lassitude.

She was being foolish, she chided herself. After all, she was quite alone here and would be for some time. Why not make herself comfortable? With a brisk, determined nod, she reached down and removed her shoes, then reached behind her to undo the buttons at the back of her gown. After struggling out of the wet dress, she brought a chair closer to the fire and spread the dress over its back.

Wearing only her low-cut chemise, she used the silk table covering to dry herself as thoroughly as she could. When she finished, she let the cloth fall to the floor, spreading her arms and closing her eyes as she felt the delicious warmth first on her bare shoulders and scantily covered breasts and then, when she turned, on her back. Tired, her head nodding involuntarily, she jerked back to wakefulness with an effort.

If only she could rest for a few minutes, she thought, she would soon be herself again. As she walked away from the fire, planning to search the dark recesses of the room for a comfortable chair, she stepped, by chance, on the bearskin rug. Feeling its silken softness underfoot, she wriggled her toes.

Tempted, Deirdre knelt on the rug and ran her hand across its smooth surface. With a weary sigh she gave in to temptation, lying full length on her side on the black fur, at first facing the warmth of the blazing logs, then turning onto her back and stretching her arms languorously above her head.

Fighting off sleep, she reached out and retrieved the silk table covering. Shifting onto her side again, she curled into a ball, pulling the silk cloth over her and then hugging herself. Closing her eyes, she smiled expectantly as she allowed her thoughts to wander, imagining herself with Clive in a small boat, her hand trailing in the water as they drifted down a slow-moving stream. The summer sun shone warmly on her face and the scent of roses filled the air . . .

*She was with Clive, the two of them alone together deep in one of the mossy recesses of the glen with the sun glimmering through the branches over her head to dapple the forest floor. Clive was stroking her back, his hand gentle as his fingers traced a succession of ever smaller circles on her bare skin. She realized she should be outraged by what Clive*

121

*was doing, shocked by this intimacy, yet she was not; the caresses seemed right and proper just as long as they were Clive's.*

*An exquisite warmth flowed upward through her body and she sighed with pleasure. I love Clive Chadbourne, she told herself. I have always loved him and I always will, now and forevermore, regardless of whether he loves me or not. His hand left her back and her breath caught as tears welled in her eyes. He had never loved her and he never would, she told herself ruefully as her sense of loss brought a lump to her throat.*

*And then he touched her again, his fingers sliding upward along her back. She felt his warm breath on her ear as he whispered her name. "Deirdre, Deirdre, Deirdre." His fingers found the nape of her neck and he caressed her there while he said her name over and over again.*

*His hand trailed across her bare skin to her shoulder, the pressure of his fingers gently urging her to turn to him, to come to him. She turned slowly, unafraid, and suddenly his lips were hard on hers, his chest pressed to her breasts.*

Her eyes flew open in shocked realization that this was real, this was not a dream. She stared at him in horror. This was not Clive who held her, but Edward!

Deirdre clutched his hair in her hand and yanked hard, hearing him gasp in pain. She screamed as she wrenched herself free. He drew back, releasing her, and she sprang to her feet, leaving him entangled in the silk cloth. She snatched her gown from the chair and held it with both hands in front of her.

As she stared at him in horror, Edward thrust the cloth aside and slowly pushed himself up from the floor, his gaze never leaving her. The firelight glittered from his brown eyes. He was naked to the waist. This must be a nightmare, Deirdre told herself, her heart pounding in fear.

Edward took a menacing step toward her and she screamed again.

"No one can possibly hear you," he said. His face was flushed and she could hear his short, sharp intakes of breath.

He held out his hand to her as though inviting her to come to him. "You wanted me, Deirdre," he said, "I could tell you wanted me when I touched you, when I caressed you. How can you possibly deny it?"

She shook her head. "No, I never did. Never. Not you."

"You flaunted yourself before me, Deirdre. Everyone saw you. Quite without shame. You came with me to the pantheon. Here, to this room. Alone."

Still shaking her head, she backed away from him until her groping hand touched the wall behind her. He came toward her and stopped, his face shadowed. Suddenly he took her head between his hands and leaned forward to kiss her. Still clutching the damp gown, she put her hands between them, her palms spread on the bare flesh of his chest, and tried to push him away.

Unexpectedly, he whirled to one side. She stared in confusion, saw another figure, hand outstretched, behind Edward. A man's hand. Clive! Edward stepped away from both of them. Clive peeled the glove from his right hand, held it like a whip, and slapped Edward across the face.

Edward blinked and his cheeks flushed with anger, but he shook his head. "Do you actually intend to throw down the gauntlet to me?" he asked, his voice unnaturally calm. "I have no quarrel with you, Chadbourne. This is no affair of yours."

When Clive raised the glove to strike Edward again, the image of two duelists flashed into Deirdre's mind, Clive and Edward, facing one another in the misty dawn with pistols raised. No, she thought, no, no, no.

Edward held up his hands, fingers spread wide in a placating gesture. "If you insist on an affair of honor," he said, "then of course you shall have one. Consider this, though, Chadbourne: the reason for our encounter will soon be known and, no matter who prevails, the end result will be to ruin this young lady, ruin her completely." He nodded toward Deirdre.

Clive hesitated. With an exclamation of disgust, he hurled the glove to the floor and clenched his hand into a fist, swung, and struck Edward on the side of the face. Edward staggered back, reaching behind him to grasp a chair only to overturn it. Clive advanced on him, hit him again, hard and full in the face, and Deirdre saw blood spurt from Edward's nose.

With a snarl of rage, Edward assumed the time-honored boxing position, standing upright with his fists raised. He jabbed at Clive, a stinging blow to the chest followed by a sharp blow to the stomach.

Clive advanced as Edward danced away from him, his tongue licking blood from his mouth, then stepped forward to jab again, this time to Clive's head, again to his body. Clive swung and his sweeping blow, partly blocked by Edward's upraised hand, glanced off Edward's forehead.

Edward, Deirdre realized, was the more skillful boxer, while Clive had the advantage of his greater height and strength, although, she feared, he had been weakened by his wound. Deirdre glanced quickly about her, looking for something, anything—a candlestick? a lamp?—to use to help Clive. Edward had outraged her; she hated him, she wanted to hurt him. However, she saw nothing.

Edward dropped his hands to his sides. "Do whatever you will," he said to Clive, smiling weakly.

Clive drew back his fist. Deirdre held her breath. Refusing to strike the defenseless Edward, Clive turned on his heel and stood facing away from his opponent. Without looking at him, Clive muttered, "Get out."

Edward bowed slightly to Clive's back. "I have just remembered that I have urgent business requiring my presence in town," he said, "and I must leave Harmon Hall at once. I assure you I shall say nothing about what happened here today. Not now, not ever."

Clive nodded without responding.

Edward glanced at Deirdre and started to speak, but seemed to think better of it, swinging around and leaving the room, leaving not through the door—the key was still in the lock where she had inserted it—but by way of an opening in one of the paneled walls.

Clive turned to Deirdre, who stood holding her gown to cover her near-nakedness. In the semidarkness, she was unable to read his expression. Disappointment? Anger? Something more? Consumed by shame, she flushed as she lowered her head.

"Deirdre, look at me," Clive demanded.

She raised her eyes to meet his gaze.

He spoke only one word, hurling it at her in disgust. "Harlot!

## Chapter Eleven

"Get dressed," Clive ordered. Turning his back to Deirdre, he folded his arms across his chest.

Angry tears burned her eyes. How dared he insult her! As she hastily donned her damp, impossibly wrinkled gown, she found her anger mingling with a hurt that struck deep into her heart. How could Clive believe, even for an instant, that she had been guilty of anything?

Buttoning her gown up the back as best she could, she slipped on her shoes and tied the ribbons of her bonnet under her chin. Her gloves were nowhere to be seen. Glancing at Clive, she drew in a deep breath. Shamed by his finding her alone with Edward, pained and stung by his accusation, she felt the need to gather her courage before she tried to actually face him.

When at last she hesitantly went to stand beside him, Clive refused either to look at her or to acknowledge her presence.

"I *did* scream for help," she pointed out.

"I heard you."

His clipped words told her he was unwilling to

say anything more than was absolutely necessary. How he must despise her. Without good reason. She had gone with Edward only to help Clive, but he could not be expected to realize the truth. Nor could she tell him. Even so, he had no right to berate her.

"How ever did you happen to come here and find me?" she asked. While curious to hear his answer, she was also determined to force him to talk to her. She absolutely refused to attempt to explain her behavior until he apologized for that offensive name he had called her, but she was also unwilling to suffer in silence.

Adamantly refusing to look at her, he said, "When Vincent and I arrived somewhat belatedly at the picnic, Sybil informed me she observed you rowing down the river with that bas—" He caught himself. "With your great good friend Edward."

"And you followed us?" She failed to keep her surprise from her voice. What, she asked herself, had prompted Clive to do that?

He hunched his shoulders, appearing flustered. "The bad weather," he said. "I was worried you might be caught on the river by the storm, so I walked downstream along the shore. When the rain began, I became even more alarmed. After coming upon the rowboat tied to the dock, I followed the path to the pantheon, where I searched in the rotunda for some sign of you until I finally saw your parasol leaning against the wall."

Could he have been jealous of Edward's attentions toward her? Deirdre wondered. Although unlikely, the possibility both intrigued and emboldened her. "And all to be certain I had found shelter from the rain," she said, with more than a touch of asperity. "Yet I seem to recall you were not overconcerned when, more than once, we were caught in the rain in Ashdown Forest."

Sighing in exasperation, Clive slowly turned to face her, looking down at her with his dark eyes flashing and his barely healed scar a red slash against skin darkened by his flush of anger. "If you must know, Deirdre, I was more concerned for your reputation, not to mention your virtue, than because of any fear you might be caught in the storm. As *you* should have been, but evidently were not, not in the least. You must have been aware of Edward's questionable reputation; everyone else in London was from the time he returned from Canada. If not before."

Even as she felt a glow of embarrassment suffuse her cheeks, she said, her voice rising, "And you, of course, assumed I would be totally unable to cope with Edward if the need arose."

"You? Cope? Ha! When your scream led me to the secret entrance to this room, your attempt at coping with Edward, if that is how you choose to describe what you were doing, appeared to me to be rather unsuccessful." He stared accusingly at her. "Or is it possible I misinterpreted the situation? Perhaps your state of dishabille was a deliberate ploy on your part."

She gasped. How dare he! She would not tolerate another insult. Drawing back her hand, she slapped his face as hard as she could.

Clive blinked. Again she drew back her hand, but

before she could slap him again, he reached out and grasped her wrist. She looked up at him, read anger in his smoldering eyes and something more, a strange, dark fire that caused her to catch her breath.

He stood holding her wrist, his gaze meeting hers, the firelight glittering in his brown eyes, his lips slightly parted. For an instant he seemed to be inviting her to come to him and, yes, she was certain (or was she?), to kiss him, but she stood as though frozen and then the moment passed and his hand dropped from her wrist and he closed his eyes, sighed, and shook his head.

He swung away from her and began to pace back and forth in front of the fireplace. "Pray forgive me, Deirdre," he said at last. "Somehow you have the knack of causing me to completely forget myself. One moment I want to keep you out of harm's way, the next I find myself upbraiding you." He stopped pacing and, standing a considerable distance from her, said, "Will you forgive me? Forgive me for everything I may have said or done?"

Her anger fled as quickly as it had come and her wounded heart healed instantly. Forgive him? She would forgive Clive anything. Nodding, she said, "Of course I forgive you."

At the same time, belatedly, she realized she had never thanked him for rescuing her from Edward's unwanted attentions, for saving her from a terrible embarrassment, at the least, or a much more dire fate, at the worst. Trying to make amends, she said, "I should have thanked you for following me here rather than questioning your motives. I admit I misjudged Edward, I should never have come here with him."

"Perhaps, Deirdre, you were trying to prove you were no longer a child."

Did Clive mean she wanted to prove it to *him?* No, that was not true, the notion had never entered her head, not once. She frowned. Could she possibly have been guilty of what he suspected without realizing it?

As though aware she might have misconstrued his words, he hastily added, "Prove it to everyone, not only to me."

"You always did see me as a child, you always treated me like a child, and that was all very well when I *was* a child, but you still insist on thinking of me as your little sister." Deirdre shook her head. "But no, I had nothing to prove, not to you or to anyone else. I went with Edward because—"

She stopped abruptly. How could she possibly tell Clive that her intent had been to distract Edward from what both she and Alcida saw as his pursuit of Phoebe? With Phoebe's acquiescence. If she did tell him the truth, Clive would either refuse to believe her or, if she did succeed in convincing him, his questions would force her to reveal the reasons for her doubts about Phoebe's faithfulness. Which she would never do.

"Because?" Clive demanded, echoing her word. "Is it possible Edward enticed you to go with him by promising a high wind and more kites for you both to fly?"

Where had he heard about their kite-flying in the park? Deirdre wondered. And why had he been nettled into sarcasm by the thought of her and Edward being together? "He promised no kites," she said. "I went with him on a random impulse, a mere whim."

"As a mouse might impulsively accompany a cat, little sister?"

"I am *not* your little sister, I never have been your little sister, and I never want to be your little sister." Tears stung her eyes. No one could make her angrier than Clive.

He put his thumb and forefinger to his chin while his speculative gaze slowly roamed from the crown of her water-stained and dreadfully misshapen bonnet to the sorry curves of her gown down to the tips of her discolored shoes. "You force me to concede you are neither—" He stopped. "Are you crying, Deirdre?" Genuine concern threaded through his voice. "Have I somehow—?"

Shaking her head, Deirdre turned from him to hide her unbidden, unsuppressible tears. She heard him take a step toward her and when she felt his hand lightly touch her arm her pulses quickened. She wanted to turn to him, she wanted him to put his arms around her as he held her and comforted her, she longed to nestle her face against his chest while he told her that he believed in her, while he assured her she had done nothing wrong and promised to protect her from all harm.

Clasping her arms tightly about herself, Deirdre drew in a tremulous breath as she once more reminded herself that Clive was betrothed to Phoebe. Since he would one day marry Phoebe, she could never again turn to him or expect comfort from him except as a sister or a sister-to-be. The time to banish her foolish daydreams of herself and Clive had not only arrived but was long past.

She dabbed at her eyes with a rain-dampened handkerchief. "The rig from Harmon Hall will be here soon," she said.

"Yes, we should wait at the top of the steps."

When he handed her the shawl, now almost dry, she draped it over her shoulders. As she waited for him to unlock the door, she glanced at one of the pictures on the wall nearest her, a scene in black and white of a fox pursued by baying hounds and eager hunters. Looking more closely, she saw that the larger figures were created by a combination of many tiny inked drawings artfully arranged.

Deirdre gasped. The small drawings, there must have been hundreds of them, depicted naked men, women, and even animals engaged in a shocking variety of strange and disgusting acts. Though she looked away at once, her face flushed a vivid red.

Clive, who had unlocked and opened the door, asked, "What is it?" When she failed to answer, he looked past her at the drawing. At first he merely frowned, but then his eyebrows shot up. He glanced at her and then looked quickly away.

Deirdre closed her eyes as the taste of bile rose in her throat. Men were vile; she hated all of them. She despised Edward, who had brought her here. And Clive, who had falsely accused her of being a wanton. Men were selfish, thinking only of satisfying their senses, seeking to gratify themselves with their endless round of reckless gambling, their drinking to all hours and to excess, their bits of muslin. She wanted nothing to do with men, ever again.

Pushing past a startled Clive, she bolted through the open door and, half walking, half running, hurried along the hallway. She heard a splintering crash behind her. Had Clive taken the picture from the wall and smashed it over the back of a chair? Men always seemed to think wrongs could be righted by breaking things.

When she entered the great rotunda of the pantheon, Deirdre looked between the soaring marble columns and saw that, though the rain had lessened, it still fell steadily in a drizzling mist. There was no sign of the promised rig.

"Deirdre," Clive called from somewhere behind her.

Deirdre looked around her, seeking a place to hide, finally running to the farthest of the pillars, standing with her back to its far side where Clive would not see her. Tired, drained of all emotion, she stared numbly at the shrouded wraiths of the trees and at the river beyond, its far shore invisible in the rain. Curling wisps of mist dampened her face, and she shivered.

"Deirdre." She heard Clive's footfalls on the marble floor, now closer, now farther away.

If only the rig would come! She longed to be alone in her misery, wanted to put as much distance between herself and the pantheon as she could, wanted to be far away from Clive. Even Clive.

She closed her eyes, remembering being a child and snuggling in bed, warm and safe, as her grandmother read her a bedtime story of a little girl living among elves and fairies in an enchanted forest where good witches brewed magic potions.

"Deirdre." Startled, her eyes flew open and she saw Clive standing but a few feet away, watching her. She turned her back to him.

"Deirdre," he said again, pleading with her. Though tempted to answer, she forced herself to ignore him.

Without warning, he grasped her arm and roughly spun her around to face him, grasped her other arm, holding and shaking her. "Deirdre," he said once more, his voice harsh.

Her breath caught.

"Deirdre," he said after a moment, his voice suddenly soft and tender.

She looked up at him, at his shadowed face, at his hair glistening from the mist, at his dark eyes. Her hand reached to him without her willing it, her fingers gently touching the scar on his temple. His eyes darkened and narrowed, he leaned closer.

"No," she whispered, shaking her head as her heart pounded wildly. "No, Clive, no," she said, not sure what she meant to deny him, the words instinctive.

His grip on her arms relaxed. She felt his hands slide behind her back, enclosing her, gathering her into his embrace, drawing her to him even though her hands were on his chest, pushing him away. Her gaze met his and she gasped when she saw the fire in his brown eyes, the need, the wanting, the passion.

Deirdre gasped. Seemingly of their own volition, her hands left his chest to slide around his body. In an instant she was in his arms. His hand found the nape of her neck, his fingers caressing her, his touch sending shivers coursing up and down her spine. His mouth came to hers and she closed her eyes as his lips brushed hers as lightly as a whisper, lips touching lips and then leaving only to return to touch again and again.

He cried out, his inarticulate cry akin to a surrender, and his arms tightened about her, crushing her body to his so that she felt the long, hard length of him, his thighs to her thighs, his chest to her breasts, and he kissed her, a demanding kiss, a kiss seeking, seeking, and then finding a response as she kissed him in return, surrendering herself to him for a long moment, a moment when he, Clive, became her world, a secret closed world of their own, the two of them alone together.

His lips left hers. He stepped back, staring down at her. Deirdre's breath came in short, ragged gasps; her heart pounded. She desperately tried to regain her composure, but failed.

Clive shook his head. "Pray forgive me, Deirdre," he said. "I quite forgot myself."

Forgive him? Anger welled up in her; she reddened. Forgive him? Because he forgot himself? Her thoughts tumbled over one another in a confused jumble. Did Clive believe he had forced himself on her, kissed her against her will? Or did he suspect she had enticed him into kissing her as he had accused her of enticing Edward? Forgive him? If he meant for kissing her, there was no reason to forgive him for that. For his ready apology, though, she would never forgive him . . . never.

Had he lost all respect for her? Had finding her with Edward caused him to think she could be trifled with and then mollified with an apology?

"I—I—" Words failed her. She stepped to him, not knowing what she intended to do, and found herself beating on his chest with her fists.

Clive backed away, staring at her in blank amazement. "Deirdre," he said, "what is it? What have I done?"

Her hands dropped to her sides. How she wished she were elsewhere, miles from Clive. "Nothing," she told him. "Nothing at all."

Hearing the thudding of hooves, she glanced toward the driveway and to her relief saw the black outline of the promised rig appear out of the rain and fog.

The driver, a thin, black-haired youth, looped the reins and sprang to the ground. Opening the door to the carriage, he bowed and stood waiting until Deirdre walked down the steps of the pantheon. Clive hastened after her. When he attempted to take her arm to help her into the carriage, she abruptly drew away from him and climbed the steps unaided. Once they were both inside, she sat as far from him as she possibly could.

She had only been trying to help Clive, Deirdre reminded herself. With what disastrous results! Edward had betrayed her and Clive had castigated her, accusing her of being a harlot and then, adding insult to injury, had taken advantage of her affection for him.

Deirdre nodded her head emphatically. Gentlemen (such a misnomer!) of the *ton,* including Clive

Chadbourne, could not be trusted. She should have realized before this that London was not the place for her. While she had come to accept and even like her stepmother, her only real friend in the city was Alcida. She would miss her younger stepsister, but her mind was made up; she would leave London as soon as possible and go home to East Sussex and the one person in the world who truly loved her, the only person she could really trust, her grandmother.

## Chapter Twelve

"How very mysterious it seemed to all of us," Alcida said to Deirdre. "You and Edward went boating on the Thames, but later you returned to Harmon Hall not with Edward, but escorted by Clive, while Edward left the Hall, completely disappeared from view and, to the best of my knowledge, has not been seen again either in town or in the country. I do hope no harm has befallen him."

Since the day was uncommonly mild for early November, the two sisters were taking the air in the park across from the Darrington house.

"I expect Edward is quite well," Deirdre said, rather more tartly than she had intended, "and will reappear when it suits his fancy to do so." Although she found it difficult, Deirdre did her best to keep her anger at Edward concealed, even from Alcida.

"Phoebe is even more puzzled than I am by what happened at the Hall," Alcida said. "As you and I were both aware, Edward had been paying considerable attention to her despite her betrothal, and I suspect she considered him to be one of her many conquests. So she must have suffered gall and wormwood to have you be the center of attention both at the picnic and afterward."

"There is absolutely nothing for either of you to be puzzled about," Deirdre said, "since the entire matter is easily explained. After the three of us—Edward, myself, and Clive—sought shelter from the rain in the pantheon, Edward told us he had been summoned to town on a matter of great urgency, and Clive was kind enough to offer to escort me back to the Hall. I fail to find what happened either puzzling or mysterious."

This had been her account of the incident from the very beginning and, since it was the truth as far as it went, which, she was forced to admit to herself, was not a very great distance, Deirdre was able to relate it without feeling too uncomfortable or finding herself entangled in the revealing contradictions that were so often the residue of lies.

"Poor, dear Clive," Alcida said. "Vincent tells me he continues to struggle against his despondency but with little success. I do wish Phoebe would agree to set a date for their wedding, instead of keeping him dangling."

"Perhaps Phoebe is having second thoughts about marriage, whether to Clive or to someone else. I suspect Phoebe may be coming to realize no man, Clive included, can be trusted." If Phoebe had not, Deirdre told herself, she most certainly should.

Alcida gave her sister a sharp glance. "Why," she said, "whatever do you mean? I never heard you speak so bitterly before, so cynically. Surely gentle-

140

men are no better or worse than women."

"I fear the books you read, Alcida, give you a false picture of men. Few if any men, at least those of my acquaintance, resemble the heroes of literature. They care for no one but themselves, they seek only the gratification of their senses."

"Not Clive Chadbourne. And certainly not Vincent. Can you possibly imagine a kinder, gentler, more thoughtful man than Dr. Leicester?"

"What you say only proves the truth of the proverb: love is blind. Not," Deirdre hastened to add, "that I have any reason to think ill of Dr. Leicester. He may well possess all the virtues you claim for him."

Alcida reddened. "Love? How did you—?"

She looked quickly away, her face hidden by her parasol. When she turned to Deirdre, tears were glistening in her eyes. "I do love Vincent," she admitted. "I love him with all my heart." Alcida shook her head sadly. "And he cares not one whit for me. How could he, when every time he looks at me—?" Her fingers ran along her scarred cheek, brushing away her tears. "Oh, Deirdre," she cried, "how miserable I am. What am I to do?"

Deirdre took Alcida in her arms and hugged her. What could she tell her sister? How could she comfort her when Alcida's fears were probably justified? No man could be trusted to see past a scarred face to a kind and loving heart. "There will be someone for you," she whispered, "someday. I promise you there will."

Alcida drew in a deep breath and stepped back. "I will try to believe," she said dully, without conviction, "that there will be somebody, someday. Oh, Deirdre, what would I ever do without you?"

Deirdre felt a sharp pang of guilt. Only the evening before, she had written to her grandmother, suggesting she be invited to East Sussex for the Christmas holiday—a short visit that Deirdre hoped she would be able to extend indefinitely.

"You would do very well without me," Deirdre said, even as she wondered what the future might hold for Alcida. Would she become, as she evidently feared, a spinster? There were worse fates, Deirdre told herself.

"I detest self-pity," Alcida said, as they started back to the Darrington house. Attempting a smile, she changed the subject. "Did I tell you I was re-reading *Castle Rackrent*, one of Maria Edgeworth's Irish tales, a most lively and rewarding novel and therefore certain to raise my spirits? Men may disappoint, but books seldom do."

They left the park, Deirdre locking the gate behind them, just as a young gentleman of the *ton*, a stranger to Deirdre, drove by in his curricle. He glanced idly at the two sisters, touched his hat, and looked away and then back again to stare at Deirdre. As they walked across the cobbled street, Deirdre noticed that the young man was on his way around the square and, as they climbed the steps to the Darrington house, he drove past them again, a great deal more slowly this time, his gaze fixed on Deirdre.

"Who can he be?" Alcida asked after they entered the house. "Are you acquainted with him? I suspect you have attracted a secret admirer."

142

Deirdre shook her head. "He might possibly have been at the Harmon ball," she said, "but I have no recollection of dancing with him or speaking to him or even seeing him, none at all."

"How strange. He stared at you as though he knew you, or thought he did and for some reason wanted to be certain." She touched Deirdre lightly on the arm. "Do you recall that elderly couple?" she asked. "When we were on our way to the outing at Harmon Hall, remember how they stared at you, much the way this young man did?"

Deirdre nodded. "Perhaps someone who makes her home in London resembles me," she suggested. "After all, there must be thousands upon thousands of young women my age living here in town."

"With your flaming red hair? And residing in Mayfair? Surely I would have noticed anyone as distinctive looking as you, Deirdre, and yet I never have."

At dinner that evening, the family offered their solutions to the mystery.

"I must agree with Deirdre," Sybil said. "She no doubt bears a resemblance to someone, a young lady we have never met because she is newly arrived in town."

"I have a rather different notion," Roger Darrington said. "Is it possible that the elderly couple and the young man have all seen Deirdre in East Sussex, perhaps recently, perhaps some years ago, and now are surprised to find her here in London?"

"In my opinion," Phoebe put in, "the entire matter is nothing more than a figment of my two sisters' over-lively imaginations. They have succeeded

143

in transforming the idle glances of strangers, probably occasioned by nothing more than the sight of Deirdre's unruly red hair, into enraptured stares."

Alcida shook her head. "It was *not* my imagination," she protested with uncommon fervor.

Phoebe, rising from the table, tossed her head in dismissal. "I myself have been the object of many stares and sidelong glances," she said, "but I have *never* seen fit to make them a subject for dinner table discussion." She walked away from the table.

"Phoebe!" Sybil called after her.

Phoebe turned in the doorway, obviously surprised at her mother's harsh tone.

"Phoebe," Sybil said, more softly, "I consider your remarks both unkind and uncalled for. You will apologize to your sisters at once."

Alcida stared across the table at her mother, mouth agape, glanced at Deirdre, then looked at Phoebe. Her father, Deirdre noted, gave Sybil a slight nod, leaving her with the impression that he was not at all surprised by his wife's reprimand; that he might, in fact, have had something to do with it.

Phoebe started to speak, but stopped, and for a moment Deirdre expected her to flounce defiantly from the room. Instead, she nodded to Deirdre and Alcida. "If my attempt at truth-telling inadvertently wounded either of you," she said, "I most certainly apologize."

Alcida leaned to Deirdre. "She means not a word of it," she whispered.

Phoebe expects too much, Deirdre thought, admiration—nay, adulation—wealth, social position; she sees all these things and much, much more as her due in life. Since few people ever acquired all they wanted, Phoebe would suffer until she lowered her sights.

"To my way of thinking," Alcida went on, speaking so only Deirdre could hear, "Phoebe has a mean and nasty spirit, pure and simple. I can still recall Phoebe giving herself airs and ordering me about when I was small, making me fetch and carry for her if I wanted to be rewarded by her companionship."

Phoebe did make herself difficult to like, Deirdre admitted to herself, but Deirdre still, despite all the slights and put-downs she had received from Phoebe, felt a sympathy for her stepsister that she was unable to explain. If only Phoebe were less beautiful, Deirdre told herself, and not so spoiled, her expectations might not be so high. And Phoebe might be a much happier and more contented young lady.

Later that evening, as Deirdre was on her way to her bedchamber, she heard someone playing the pianoforte in the music room. Looking in from the doorway, she saw Phoebe at the keyboard, softly singing the sad strains of Clive's favorite song, "Jamie Douglas."

> *Fare thee well, Jamie Douglas!*
> *Fare thee well, my ever dear to me!*
> *Fare thee well, Jamie Douglas,*
> *Fare thee well . . .*

The song, Deirdre recalled, was the lament of a

young woman cruelly abandoned by her wealthy Scottish husband. It represented, she told herself, thinking of Edward's betrayal, a warning that most women failed to heed: men were not to be trusted.

Deirdre, on an impulse, went into the music room, and sat unobserved until Phoebe finished the last stanza of the ballad. "Such a sad, sad song," she said softly, so as not to unduly startle her stepsister. With a slight start of her own, she realized that she had come to consider Alcida her sister while she continued to think of Phoebe as merely a stepsister.

Phoebe played a few dissonant chords before turning on the piano bench to look at Deirdre. "Mercy," she said coolly, "here we have the young lady who attracts so much attention from passing strangers. And also the last person to see Edward before his sudden disappearance from Harmon Hall. I wonder if you just happened to say something to him that caused him to leave so abruptly."

What could Phoebe have in mind? "I think not," Deirdre said.

"He was quite amiable and certainly attentive while the two of us were nutting, never hinting at business in town, and then, later, he left without a word to anyone except you and Clive. Is it possible you cast some aspersions on me, spun some lurid tale from your fertile imagination for his benefit?"

Deirdre was outraged. "I most certainly did nothing of the sort. I never discussed you with Edward, I never have, and I never will."

"I wonder. If what you claim is true, his rude behavior toward me is quite inexplicable."

Deirdre quelled her annoyance and leaned forward, eager to do whatever she could to make peace. "Phoebe," she pleaded, "when I came to live here, I hoped we could become friends, if not at first, then in time. Can we? Will you allow me to be your friend?"

"But we are friends as well as sisters." Phoebe smiled coldly. "Your father says we are, my mother agrees with him, as she is wont to do, and so we must be friends, the very best of friends."

Deirdre stood and, too angry and exasperated to answer, walked to the door, where she turned to look at Phoebe. "A friendly word of warning," she said. "Edward is everything they accuse him of being. For all his wealth and charm, all his compliments and other pleasantries, Edward is a rake and not to be trusted."

Phoebe rose slowly from the piano bench. "And how," she demanded, "did you come by this intimate knowledge of Edward's character? Is it possible, Deirdre, that after dangling for him and failing to land him, you lowered your opinion of him? Could it be, Deirdre, that you have failed to tell us everything that occurred during your visit to the pantheon?"

Sorry she had spoken, Deirdre said, "I thought I should warn you about Edward, for your sake. Whether you heed the warning or not is up to you."

Phoebe crossed the room to Deirdre. "The reason for your so-called warning is quite obvious to me," she said in a low, intense voice. "You, Deirdre, are obviously jealous. Of me. From the first day you came into this house, you envied me. In the beginning, because of Clive Chadbourne, because you wanted Clive for yourself and were devastated when he chose me."

Deirdre, realizing the hopelessness of talking rationally to Phoebe, shook her head. "I was never envious of you," she said.

"You may shake your head as much as you wish and deny the truth time after time, but I can tell from the guilt written on your face how right I am. And then, after you lost Clive to me, there was Edward. You noticed him being attentive to me and you decided to try your best to entice him away from me by wearing that disgraceful gown to the picnic at Harmon Hall."

Deirdre could only shake her head in denial.

"Everyone was either aghast when they saw you," Phoebe went on, "or they were laughing at you behind your back. You never realized that, did you, Deirdre? And when you failed to entrap Edward with your wiles, you must have told him something about me that caused him to leave the Hall without a word of explanation."

"Goodnight, Phoebe." Deirdre whirled around and walked to the stairs.

"Everyone at the picnic was laughing at you," Phoebe called after her . . .

I belong in East Sussex, not here in London, Deirdre told herself as she lay in bed, waiting impatiently for sleep to come. On the other hand, Phoebe had thrown down the gauntlet to her, and to leave town now would seem like an ignominious retreat, would mean giving a gloating Phoebe sole possession of the field of battle. And she would be deserting poor Alcida, leaving her without a champion, without a friend.

How impossibly self-centered Phoebe was, believing whatever happened to Edward or anyone else must be because of her, because of Miss Phoebe Langdon, the only person who deserved to be the center of attention in all of the known world as well as in the *terra incognito,* a young lady who buttressed her belief in her own importance with complicated tales of betrayal concocted from truths, half-truths, and complete fabrications.

How could she ever come to think of such a schemer as her sister? Deirdre asked herself. And yet her grandmother always insisted that good lay within every heart, good that would eventually make itself known if only one was patient enough. Was that true? Clive, despite what he had done, meant well. But how could she ever forgive Edward's atrocious behavior? Or explain away Phoebe's cruel and unjust taunts?

I must not allow her to upset me, Deirdre told herself, even as she admitted that, from time to time, Phoebe's barbs struck distressingly close to her heart. What shall I do? she wondered. Shall I stay here or go home to East Sussex? she asked herself as she slipped into sleep, little realizing that the question would be answered for her within the next twenty-four hours. In a quite startling and dramatic fashion.

The three sisters and Sybil were alone in the house the next afternoon, Mr. Darrington having

149

business with his solicitor in the City, when Clive Chadbourne was announced. Clive, Deirdre noted with a rush of hope, looked more buoyant than she had seen him since his return to England. No matter what had passed between them, she longed for him to recover from his terrible experience in battle.

"Do you recall," he said to Alcida, after a hurried and perfunctory exchange of pleasantries, "a conversation you and I had while at Harmon Hall?"

Alcida, flustered at being singled out, shook her head.

"You must remember," Clive persisted. "It concerned something that happened here in town when you and Deirdre entered your carriage on your way to the Hall."

Alcida nodded. "I recall telling you about an elderly couple staring and nodding at Deirdre as if they recognized her." When Clive started speak, she added, "In fact, we had a very similar experience only yesterday." She glanced at Phoebe as though expecting her sister to again suggest her story was more imagination than fact, but Phoebe merely raised her eyebrows expressively.

"With the same couple?" Clive asked.

"No, this time a young man driving a curricle made a circuit of the park so he could return for a second look at Deirdre."

Clive nodded. "Just so, Alcida. I am surprised, not at the two occurrences you describe, but because there have not been many more. At all events, last evening I solved the puzzle. I now know why Deirdre has attracted the attention of strangers on the streets of Mayfair and, if you four ladies will be kind enough to don your wraps and accompany me, I shall be most happy to take you where you will be able to witness the explanation of the mystery with your own eyes."

## Chapter Thirteen

"Where are we bound?" Phoebe asked, as Clive's traveling chaise turned into Swallow Street.

"To Queen Anne Street," he told her.

"Queen Anne?" she echoed. "We have no acquaintances there."

"Quite right," Clive said. "Neither your family nor I do."

"Then why—?" Phoebe began.

"The answer to that question must wait until we arrive at Queen Anne Street. My surprise would be a great disappointment, in fact would be no surprise at all, if I revealed it now."

They rode on in an expectant though puzzled silence until the chaise stopped in front of a respectable though not grand house on a street of other respectable though not grand houses. As they stepped down from the carriage, Deirdre saw a couple entering the house nod to two gentlemen who were leaving.

Deirdre pulled her paisley shawl tightly around her to ward off the chill of the north wind sweeping down the street and, accompanied by Sybil and Alcida, followed Clive and Phoebe along the walkway to the house. One of the departing gentlemen, florid-faced and graying, glanced at her casually, blinked, and then stared, open-mouthed. When she frowned, he looked away, evidently embarrassed.

Rather than using the bell pull, Clive opened the door himself and ushered them inside. Once in the front hall, Deirdre was surprised to find no one, neither servant nor host, to greet them.

"I suggest we all keep our wraps on," Clive said, "since unfortunately the heating here is practically nonexistent. The housekeeping, I fear, also leaves a great deal to be desired. Of course, we came not for warmth, nor to view a well-ordered household."

Why *have* we come here? Deirdre wondered.

Clive led them down a long hallway where, some distance ahead of them, Deirdre saw people coming and going through an open door to one of the rooms. As they drew nearer, she heard the hum of conversation, and when they came to the doorway, she looked inside and saw a crush of gaily bonneted ladies and top-hatted gentlemen of the *ton*.

Glancing over their heads, Deirdre caught her breath, for every available space on all four walls of the large room was crowded with paintings — watercolors, for the most part, but also a few oils. Several portraits were scattered amidst the many land- and seascapes on which grays, blues, and browns predominated, with here and there a contrasting swirl of red or yellow. The style of the artist — Deirdre sensed that all of the paintings were the work of one man — and the great romantic

153

sweep of sea, sky, and clouds in the pictures seemed strangely familiar.

"Over here," Clive said, mumbling excuses to right and left as he made his way through the crush toward the far end of the room.

At first his progress was greeted by growls of annoyance, but when gallery visitors looked past Clive and saw Deirdre, the muttering gradually stopped as the men and women stared as they hastened to make way for her.

"Ah, here we are," Clive announced with a smile of triumph and a sweep of his hand as the last of the crowd stepped to one side.

Deirdre gasped as she looked up at the portrait, her hand going to her breast. She felt Alcida's fingers grip her wrist while beside her Phoebe and Sybil stared in startled silence.

On the bottom of the frame of the life-sized painting, a printed legend read: "Diana, Goddess of the Chase." The portrait depicted the Roman goddess in a short green hunting dress, its hem several inches above her knees, with a brown sash emphasizing the narrowness of her waist below the fullness of her breasts. Her right hand was reaching over her shoulder to draw an arrow from a quiver she carried on her back, her other hand rested on the head of a deer leaping at her side.

There could be no doubt at all that Deirdre was the goddess and the goddess was Deirdre. The artist had faithfully captured her flaming red hair, her high cheekbones, and her green eyes.

When Clive took a paper from his pocket, unfolded it, and held it up in front of the painting,

Deirdre recognized the sketch he had taken with him to Spain. Her face in the sketch almost exactly matched that of the portrait.

"Wherever did you find that?" Phoebe asked, looking at him askance.

"It was a gift from Mr. Turner," Deirdre said, "the artist Clive and I met at the bridge in Ashdown Forest last summer."

"Joseph William Mallord Turner, to give his full name," Clive said. "Since he put the painting on exhibition, the portrait has become the talk of the town. Especially so when Mr. Turner had to admit he had no notion who his model might be."

"How beautiful Deirdre looks in the painting," Alcida said. "Though no more beautiful than she really is."

Clive looked from Deirdre to the portrait and then back at Deirdre again. He frowned and started to speak, seemed to have second thoughts, and said nothing, but Deirdre noted a pondering look come over his face, almost as though he were viewing her in an entirely different light than he ever had before.

"I, for one," said Phoebe haughtily, "would never think of allowing a painting of myself, especially one in such revealing attire, to be placed on display in a public place where just anyone and his cousin could walk in from the street to gawk at my likeness."

Deirdre, who had at first been surprised when she saw the painting, then exhilarated and then shy, now became embarrassed, wondering if Phoebe could be right; that having her portrait on display, especially with the daring exposure of calf and knee, might not be the thing.

"I find the likeness to be quite good," Sybil said, as she looked from Deirdre to the painting. "Most men and women of quality," she said softly to Phoebe, "seem to have no objection to having their portraits exhibited in their homes, at the Royal Academy and elsewhere. To my way of thinking, Deirdre should consider it a compliment."

Deirdre felt a rush of gratitude. How kind of Sybil to take her part, she told herself; how fair-minded she seemed. As Deirdre came to know her stepmother better, she found herself liking her more and more.

"The portrait of Diana sold almost at once, I believe," an older gentleman standing near them commented, "for a sum of more than two thousand guineas. To a titled Italian collector from Milan, I was told."

"Not so," another man remarked. "The purchaser was none other than the Duke of Clarence."

"No, both of you are in error," a third gentleman maintained. "I was informed by a friend of the artist that the portrait was purchased for the Prince Regent's private collection."

The admiring crowd swirled around Deirdre. Two young peers pleaded with Clive to be introduced, an elderly gentleman presented her with a rose, a young girl shyly touched her hand and fled. Flustered by the unexpected attention, surrounded by well-wishers, she heard her name repeated whichever way she turned, "Miss Deirdre Darrington, the model is Miss Deirdre Darrington."

She noticed a tall, thin footman in green and gold livery enter the room and frown as he saw the crush. Pushing his way rather unceremoniously to her side, he murmured in her ear, "Miss Darrington?" When she nodded, he said, "The new owner of your portrait would very much like to have the privilege of meeting you." Without waiting for her reply, he started away.

Deirdre glanced about her, intending to ask Sybil to come with her, but she saw that Clive and the rest of her party were quite out of earshot. Reaching Sybil in this crush would be well-nigh impossible.

After hesitating a moment, she decided there would be little impropriety in meeting the owner, so she excused herself and followed the footman from the room. He led her farther along the hallway and turned to his right into another corridor, where he approached the first door and knocked.

"Come in." The voice from inside the room, Deirdre thought, sounded familiar, but she was unable to assign a name to it.

The footman opened the door and, bowing slightly, stood to one side. Deirdre entered the brightly lit room, heard the door close behind her. She looked around her and gasped. "You!" she cried.

Edward Fox, who had been standing in front of the cold fireplace, stepped back while at the same time holding his hands toward her with his fingers splayed in a gesture of conciliation.

"Please wait," he said when she drew away, "pray stay at least a moment until you hear me out. Even

157

the most dastardly of villains deserves the opportunity to be heard."

Backing to the door, Deirdre reached behind her, her fingers closing over the knob, all the while staring at him in confusion. Edward had purchased her portrait. Why? And now what did he want with her? She should never have come here alone, after all.

"Deirdre," he said fervently, "my only wish is to beg your forgiveness for my intolerable behavior at the Hall. I admit I completely lost all sense of propriety. Will you forgive me?"

She shook her head. She would never forgive him, she told herself, no matter what he said now, regardless of whatever excuse he might offer; his behavior had been inexcusable, beyond forgiving.

"If you find it impossible to forgive me," he went on, "will you at least listen to me? If you but pause and recall all of the circumstances, you will realize you were at least partly to blame for my behavior."

When she started to protest indignantly, he hurried on, "Not that I had any excuse whatsoever for my actions. You were blameless, completely so, and now, even if I go to my grave unforgiven, I ask you to allow me to attempt to make amends for my boorish behavior while you were my guest at Harmon Hall."

"How could you have taken me to that odious place?" Deirdre said, recalling the picture on the wall of the room in the pantheon with a grimace of distaste.

"I swear to you, I had never so much as entered that room before that day. It was furnished by an

158

impoverished cousin who we brought to live with us some years ago, little realizing how thoroughly depraved he was. This gentleman — though I hate to call him that — was an exceedingly small man who had married a widow and come to be called 'the widow's mite.' However that might be, he was the one who told me of the secret entrance, something I remembered only after I left you alone in the room. I behaved abominably, I admit it. What more do you want me to say?"

Deirdre hesitated. In all fairness, she should at least listen to him, she told herself. "Say what you have to say," she told him, "and be done with it once and for all."

He bowed his thanks. "If you would feel safer," he said with a slight smile, "I have no objection if you open the door."

She was not afraid of Edward, Deirdre told herself. She folded her arms and faced him, noticing that he appeared penitent, although that, she reminded herself, could well be merely a pose.

"You may wonder how I came to be here at Turner's gallery today," Edward said, "since I only returned to town last week after spending a fortnight or so tramping about the Lake Country, quite alone and miserable, reading aloud the verses of Wordsworth and Coleridge." He closed his eyes and said:

*The hare is running races in her mirth;*
*And with her feet she from the plashy earth*
*Raises a mist; that, glittering in the sun,*

159

*Runs with her all the way, wherever she doth*
*run.*

"That happens to be one of my favorites," he said, opening his eyes. "It comes from a poem by Mr. William Wordsworth."

Did Edward really expect her to believe he had been wandering about the countryside, reciting poetry? Deirdre wondered, almost finding herself amused at his audacity. Would he now recite lines from some obscure poet and claim them as his own?

"Several days after returning to town," he said, "I happened to see your portrait quite by chance and, bewitched and entranced, I at once entered into negotiations to purchase it. Not entirely because of sentiment, although I do happen to possess a rather sentimental nature, but as an investment."

Deirdre, arms still folded, was uncertain whether to believe him or not.

"I saw to it," Edward said, "that Chadbourne was informed yesterday that a portrait of a close friend of his had been placed on exhibit here at Queen Anne Street, thinking it more than likely he would bring you to view the painting at the earliest possible moment. And that is the chain of events that led to my being here conversing with you today."

Deirdre, deeply suspicious of his motives, asked, "For what possible purpose?"

"I wished to make atonement; I wished to be forgiven. Only once before in my life have I ever acted unselfishly, and that was many months ago in Canada; now I intend to do so a second time. For you, Deirdre."

Shaking her head, she stared at him with suspicion. What was he trying to tell her? Should she believe him, or was this another of his ploys, intended to confuse her so he could, in some way, take advantage of her? As he had tried to do once before.

"I intend to wipe the slate clean," he said, "to start afresh. I told you I fashioned the kite we flew in the park. That was a lie, since it was Cunningham, one of my grooms who happens to be far more clever with his hands, who did the actual work. I expect I told you a great many lies besides that one, since I seem to have made deceit a habit, especially since I lost my faith in God."

Was Edward demented? Deirdre asked herself, unable to make sense of his ramblings about his deceit and his loss of faith. Perhaps she should suggest he consult Dr. Leicester.

"Look at me, Deirdre," he demanded fiercely, his brown eyes glinting. "You love Clive Chadbourne," he said flatly. "Pray stop shaking your head and admit the truth of what I say."

"I—I—" she began. No, she refused to answer. What right had he to ask such an astonishing and impertinent question? None at all.

"You need not answer; your feelings are all too obvious." He sounded resigned. "I first suspected it at that unfortunate party welcoming Chadbourne home from the wars. I realized I was right when I saw the two of you together in the pantheon. The way you looked at him spoke louder than any words."

"My feelings or lack of feelings for Clive," she said stiffly, "are none of your concern."

He shrugged. "Because I suspected you loved him, I was rather puzzled when you accepted my invitation to go rowing on the Thames. I still am. Had you abandoned all hope where Chadbourne was concerned? I think not." All at once Edward struck his open palm with his fist. "I have it, I see now what you were about. You meant to make a noble sacrifice of yourself for Chadbourne's sake, intending to draw my attention away from the overly flirtatious Phoebe. Am I right?"

Deirdre turned from him and opened the door. "I refuse to listen to any more of your nonsense," she said.

He shook his head angrily. "What a fool you are, Deirdre."

She half expected him to stride to her, push her away from the door, and slam it shut, imprisoning her in this room, but he did not. Instead, he remained where he was, watching her intently.

"First you admit to deceiving me," she said, "and now you insult me."

"I speak the truth. Why do I consider your behavior foolish? Because you intend to turn your back on me, on someone who not only understands you—I assure you I do understand you, Deirdre— but also someone who, precisely because he does understand you, has the ability to help you."

"I need no help. Not from anyone, but especially not from you, Lord Lounsbury."

"But you do, Deirdre, you do. For some reason, which I admit I have great difficulty fathoming, you

162

feel a tenderness toward Clive Chadbourne, a man who is totally undeserving of you."

When she started to protest, he said, "Pray wait until I finish. Chadbourne has certain good qualities, I suppose, being handsome and heroic and all of that, but any man who would ask for the hand of Phoebe Langdon rather than Deirdre Darrington demonstrates a lack of something, call it good judgment or common sense or what-have-you."

"Phoebe is exceptionally beautiful."

Edward nodded toward a table of bric-a-brac. "And so is that blue vase, but I would hesitate to contemplate an intimate acquaintance with it. Phoebe is also inordinately selfish and self-satisfied to an astonishing degree. I happen to be a good judge of those particular characteristics since I possess both of them myself. Or I did until the last year or so, when my experience in the New World taught me a few bitter lessons."

Deirdre sighed. "I admit I like Clive. I always have, ever since we were children together in Sussex."

"That may be, but the fact remains that I, Edward Fox, Marquess of Lounsbury, would make a much better match for you, Deirdre. If, that is, you prefer a bit of excitement and a touch of uncertainty, instead of a future spent living happily ever after."

Deirdre smiled. "Do my ears deceive me, or am I listening to a proposal of marriage?" she asked, trying to suggest by her light-hearted question that they were merely bantering.

"No, you are not, since I have regretfully abandoned the field to the undeserving Chadbourne. I do, however, intend to atone for my misdeeds by being your friend, by helping you whether you wish me to or not. But before you leave this room to return to bask in the adulation of the art lovers who have flocked to Turner's gallery to view your portrait, may I give you a word of advice, or rather several words of advice?"

"I imagine you will, no matter what I may say."

"My advice is this, Deirdre: if you care for our friend Chadbourne as much as I suspect you do, you should make him aware of that fact as soon as you possibly can. I warn you, if you dither and dally much longer, as you appear wont to do, it will be too late."

## Chapter Fourteen

Following the exhibition of the portrait of Deirdre as the goddess Diana at Joseph Turner's gallery on Queen Anne Street, life changed dramatically for all of the Darrington household. Both for the better and for the worse.

An unremitting stream of visitors made their way to the house, leaving behind cards as well as invitations to musical evenings, to balls, to teas, and to a wide variety of other social affairs. Even the patronesses of Almack's saw fit to succumb, and Deirdre and, somewhat later, Phoebe, were welcomed to the Wednesday ball and supper, discovering, as one diner-out wrote:

> *If once to Almack's you belong,*
> *Like monarchs, you can do no wrong;*
> *But banished thence on Wednesday night,*
> *By Jove, you can do nothing right.*

Deirdre's sudden fame also brought its share of tribulations. Strangers stared at her while she strolled with Alcida in the park and, more annoying, she was pressed for her opinion on a variety of subjects about which she knew little or nothing.

A well-known and talented artist had painted her portrait; the exhibition of that portrait had created a sensation, a ninety days' wonder, at first not only because of the mastery of the artist, Joseph Turner, in portraying a goddess possessed with a haunting beauty, but also as a result of the mystery surrounding his unknown model, a woman whose identity was not known even to Turner himself.

After her portrait found favor with the *ton* and Deirdre was revealed as the model, however, the *ton* in its wisdom decided that Deirdre Darrington's opinions on matters of current interest were to be valued more highly than the views of persons with actual knowledge of the subjects under discussion in this, the autumn of 1813. Not only were they valued, but they were endlessly repeated with the addition of personal commentaries both pro and con.

What, she was asked while attending a showing at the National Gallery, was her opinion of the feud between Madame de Staël and Lord Byron? And did she hold Byron's poetry in high regard or did she consider him overrated?

(She knew nothing of the feud but in such matters she tended to side with the woman, even though she admitted to being an admirer of Lord Byron's verses.)

At Almack's the questions centered on Beau Brummell. Would he ever regain the esteem of the Prince Regent after asking a mutual acquaintance, in the Regent's hearing, "Who's your fat friend?" And what of the Beau's insistence that a well-dressed gentleman should wear only blacks and whites, eschewing all color?

(She doubted that Mr. Brummell would regain the Regent's favor, although she applauded his conservative sense of style.)

What did she think of the recently installed gas lines in Westminster? an elderly gentleman at an Aldrich dinner party inquired. Were they truly a scientific advance, or a fad representing a danger to life and limb?

(She considered gas lighting a genuine improvement that should help to reduce crime in the city.)

"Have you read *Pride and Prejudice?*" a fellow browser at Hatchard's inquired. "Do you consider Elizabeth Bennet the most appealing heroine to appear in English literature since Shakespeare?"

(She had and she did.)

In the beginning, Deirdre tried to resist the adulation but then she succumbed, albeit unwillingly, and was swept along on a wave of compliments from ball to party to soirée to ball while the gentlemen of the *ton* danced attendance on her.

She had to admit she enjoyed the attention for, to a slight degree, it helped keep her thoughts from returning time and again to Clive Chadbourne.

Edward had urged her to make her feelings known to Clive; in other words, he wanted her to abandon her attempt to smooth the path to the altar for Clive and Phoebe and, to phrase it bluntly, to pursue him. This, she told herself, was what a man might do, but she would not and could not.

Clive was betrothed to Phoebe and, unless she came to decide otherwise, it would be Phoebe he would marry; whether or not she, Deirdre, deemed the match suitable, or whether Edward considered the alliance to be a courting of disaster for both participants, had absolutely no bearing on the matter.

During the last week of November, her grandmother extended an invitation for a visit during the Christmas holiday and Deirdre, so eager to leave town only a short time before, debated with herself whether to accept or decline with regrets. Even if she did go, she no longer intended to remain in East Sussex after the first of the new year. London had become altogether too satisfying for her to permanently retreat to the country as once, in the depths of despair, she had wanted to do.

Life in town was proving to be exhilarating for her family as well.

Roger Darrington was, at first, taken aback when his daughter became one of the wonders of the waning days of the London year. Soon, however, he grew accustomed to his family being at the center of a whirl of activity and, at every appropriate occasion, expressed his great pride in Deirdre. He had, he said, "Always considered her an exceedingly handsome girl."

Sybil, who had always harbored a secret envy of those a rung above her in the social hierarchy and who had regretfully considered that her marriage to Roger Darrington, a love match on her part, would write finis to her dreams, was initially surprised and then overjoyed at this change for the better in her social fortunes.

Sybil's only concern came to be the possible adverse effect of Deirdre's popularity on her elder daughter. Though she genuinely loved both Phoebe and Alcida, Phoebe had always been her secret favorite, both because she was her firstborn and because, in the opinion of many, she bore a marked resemblance to her mother.

Phoebe began by being resentful of Deirdre, a resentment that showed itself in angry, caustic remarks. Soon, however, she came to accept, albeit grudgingly, her stepsister's sudden fame and even to savor the attention that came her way in its wake.

Alcida was the least changed. Awed by Deirdre's sudden popularity, she was happy for her new sister, enjoying the reflected glory, but no more than she might enjoy reading the work of one of her favorite authors. Her thoughts, though, rarely strayed far from Dr. Leicester.

She played cards with him during evenings spent at home, she danced with him at balls and assemblies and, on occasion, strolled with him in the park, but nothing in his words or demeanor gave her hope that theirs might grow into a longer-lasting and more permanent alliance.

"He talks of little except medicine," she told Deirdre with a heartfelt sigh.

Deirdre, surprised that Alcida now seemed to be hoping for what, a short time before, she had declared to be impossible, said, "He is, I do believe, exceedingly fond of you."

Alcida shook her head dispiritedly. "Never by word or deed has he given any indication of his feelings toward me. I expect, if he feels anything at all for me, it is nothing more than pity."

"No, not pity," Deirdre said, "I believe he cares for you in quite a different, deeper way. One evening the doctor may well burst in upon us, request an audience with my father, and declare himself."

That very evening, despite a dense fog that had settled over London, to their great surprise, Dr. Vincent Leicester did burst in on Alcida, Deirdre, and Phoebe as they sat reading in the drawing room. "The most extraordinary thing has happened," he told them, his face flushed with excitement.

They looked up at him expectantly.

Rather than drawing up a chair, he strode back and forth, gesticulating as he spoke. "I have just been informed in today's post," he said, taking a bulky letter from an inner pocket and holding it aloft, "of the death of my only uncle, Jacob Leicester."

"You have our deepest sympathies," Alcida said, as her sisters nodded their concurrence.

"Thank you, you all are most kind, although my grief is lessened by the fact that to me Jacob Leicester was always merely a name, an elderly gentleman I had never set eyes on. A year or two before I was born, he left England and proceeded to spend his entire adult life on the island of Jamaica in the West Indies."

What then, Deirdre wondered, was the cause of the doctor's agitation?

"In his letter," Vincent said, "Mr. Thaddeus Hightower of Hightower, Hightower, and Scofield, a Jamaican firm of solicitors, informs me that my uncle Jacob was the sole proprietor of an extensive cocoa plantation not far from Kingston, the capital of the colony."

"And you are the heir?" Alcida asked.

"Precisely. The sole heir. Jacob never married and, in his last will and testament, he left the entire property, one of the most prosperous cocoa plantations on the island, to me."

"How wonderful for you," Alcida cried.

Dr. Leicester nodded. "I was overwhelmed with gratitude at my good fortune when I received the news, completely overwhelmed." He frowned, clasped his hands behind his back, and sighed. "However," he said, "the inheritance brings significant duties and responsibilities along with it. The plantation is presently being managed by an overseer who is becoming increasingly infirm. Mr. Hightower, therefore, has advised me in the strongest possible terms to set sail for Jamaica at my earliest convenience if I wish to preserve my inheritance."

Alcida stared at him and then, her hand going to her mouth as if to conceal her dismay, murmured, "The West Indies. So far, far away."

"And do you intend to follow Mr. Hightower's advice?" Deirdre asked.

"I do, I most certainly do. Not only do I find the prospect of living, at least for a few years, in the West Indies exceedingly intriguing; I have, ever since completing my medical training in Edinburgh, had an intense interest in the possible causes of fevers and other tropical diseases. We of the medical profession have remedies for fevers but, unfortunately,

171

have little notion of their causes. Living in Jamaica would give me the opportunity to prove or disprove some of my theories on the subject."

"I would expect," Deirdre said, after glancing at the stricken Alcida, "that one might become lonely for the company of other Englishmen, not to mention Englishwomen, in such a faraway land." Not merely Englishwomen in general, she wanted to add, but one in particular.

Dr. Leicester, appearing quite oblivious to the hint, shook his head. "That, I am told," he said, "is not a problem, since there exists a large English colony on Jamaica, where besides cocoa, there are sugar and indigo plantations worked by some of the 300,000 or more slaves. The island, as you may know, was discovered by Columbus and then settled by Spaniards who killed off the inoffensive Arawak Indians and imported Africans."

Deirdre found her attention wandering as Vincent described the flora and fauna of the island and the possibility of earthquakes and hurricanes, but Alcida listened with rapt attention.

"We occupied the island in 1655," Vincent went on to tell them, "but some of the Spanish slaves ran off to the mountains and these Maroons, as they were called, fought us until only a few years ago." He rubbed his hands together, anticipating his journey to this exotic land. "Since Mr. Hightower believes time is of the essence," he said, "I intend to begin my preparations for my departure from England on the morrow."

A short time later, the doctor bade them farewell, convinced that the three sisters, although perhaps in varying degrees, shared his enthusiasm for his forth-coming voyage to the West Indies. A tender-hearted man, although not a particularly perceptive one, he would have been profoundly shocked to learn that, even as he walked through the dense and cloying fog to Oxford Street, one of the recipients of his glad tidings was crying herself to sleep.

When the doctor arrived at his lodgings, he found Clive Chadbourne waiting for him. Despite the lateness of hour, the unexpected nature of Clive's visit, and his guest's obviously troubled expression, Dr. Leicester launched into still another impassioned recital of his glorious news, repeating his description of the island and its history.

After a considerable time, he became aware that Clive, although he nodded and now and again interjected a comment, appeared distracted. Several minutes later, he deduced that the reason was not his guest's lack of interest, but some overriding concern of his own.

Dr. Leicester rose, dusted his hands, and said, "Enough about my good news," and poured two glasses of Madeira and handed one to Clive. He sat near Clive, both men facing the dying fire in the grate.

"Forgive me," the doctor said, "for becoming overly engrossed in my own prospects while neglecting my duties as a host. You appear troubled." He glanced at Clive. "Have you had a recurrence of your megrims, perhaps?"

Clive shook his head. "Earlier this evening," he said, "I had one of the most disquieting and mysterious experiences of my life."

Dr. Leicester, surprised and distressed, turned to look fully at his friend. Of late, in fact from about the time the portrait of Deirdre-Diana had been placed on exhibition, he had considered that Clive was on his way, however slowly, to a full recovery from the melancholia brought on by his experiences in Spain. Now he wondered whether he had been mistaken.

"Tell me about this disquieting experience of yours," he said, putting down his glass and leaning forward.

Clive drew a deep breath. "It was shortly after eight, and I was walking along St. James's Street where, in spite of the early hour and the bothersome fog, I encountered a considerable number of friends coming and going from White's and the other clubs.

"Suddenly an eerie quiet settled over the city, the street seemed deserted, without even a carriage passing by, and it was then I spied, perhaps a hundred or more feet ahead of me and proceeding in the same direction, a man limping through the circle of light beneath one of the street lamps. I recognized him, or at least I thought I did, as one Lieutenant Timmons, a fellow hussar who I had last seen in Spain during the battle for Vittoria."

"This Timmons was a particular friend of yours?" Dr. Leicester asked.

Clive hesitated, his hand straying to the scar on his temple. "No, not a friend. Timmons is a man I may have abandoned to the tender mercies of the French immediately after I was wounded. The man I saw this evening limped, and Timmons always

174

walked with a bounce to his step, though the limp may have been caused by a wound."

"Did this Timmons, if it was Timmons, recognize you?"

"I think he did; I fear he did. By the time I called his name several times, Timmons, if it were he, had passed once more from the lamplight into the fog; but he must have heard my footsteps, for he retraced his steps, coming into the halo of light again, and he called, 'Chadbourne?'—proving, I suppose, it was he—and I answered, 'Yes, Clive Chadbourne here."

"To my dismay, Timmons drew a sword and advanced on me in a most menacing way, disappearing into the fog again as he approached. I waited, not afraid but not knowing what to expect, and then, when he failed to appear, I walked toward him, rather warily, I must admit, and I thought I heard his footsteps, but when I called his name again there was no answer, only a hushed silence. Although I kept calling his name, he never reappeared."

The doctor frowned. Placing his hands, fingers laced, behind his head, he leaned back in his chair and looked up at the shadowed ceiling. "You have no doubt that you did see someone? No doubt at all?"

"At the time, I was certain, as certain as I am of your presence here. Now I wonder if the entire incident might have been nothing more than a hallucination." He shook his head and sighed. "Tell me what I should do."

Dr. Leicester closed his eyes. When he reopened

them, he rose and walked to stand beside Clive. "My good friend," he said, putting a hand on Clive's shoulder, "may I, speaking both as your friend and as your physician, offer a suggestion? More than a suggestion, a recommendation."

"Of course. I came here tonight seeking your advice."

"You need rest, Clive, a time to be completely by yourself, a few weeks in seclusion, if you will, away from the clamor of town, a time spent attempting to gain a new perspective on your life." He paused as though weighing alternatives. "Your eldest brother William lives in Brighton, I believe."

"He does. With his wife and three children. All of them boys.

"I propose you visit William for a few days but then, informing no one of your plans, I suggest you proceed to Chadbourne Hall in East Sussex, remaining there until you regain your peace of mind."

"And you want me to tell no one where I am? Not even Deirdre?"

"Deirdre?" the doctor echoed, his voice showing his surprise. "Surely you mean Phoebe."

"Did I say Deirdre? I meant to say Phoebe, of course." Clive bowed his head, putting his hand to his temple. "I think I see a man in the fog who threatens me with a sword, I say the name of the wrong girl. Have I lost my senses, Vincent? Have I become demented?"

# *Chapter Fifteen*

Deirdre, sitting at her dressing table in her green velvet robe, ran her brush through her hair. "Twenty-three," she murmured, "twenty-four." Hearing a tapping at her chamber door, she said, "Come in," and glanced up at the looking glass.

Alcida, her forefinger inserted in the book she carried in her hand, entered and closed the door behind her. She marched over to stand behind Deirdre, opened the book, and began to read without any preamble and in the most acid of tones:

" *'It is a truth universally acknowledged, that a single man in possession of a good fortune, must be in want of a wife.'* "

Slapping the book shut—the sound caused Deirdre to give a start—Alcida said, "The author, who for some reason declines to identify herself, happens to be mistaken, or at least the maxim introducing her novel does not hold true for Dr. Vincent Leicester. His newfound wealth, the prospect of managing his new cocoa plantation in a distant tropical land, and the possibility of closely observing colonials and natives stricken with frightful diseases, appear to satisfy all his wants."

Deirdre, responding to Alcida's bitterness with compassion, swung about on her low-backed chair and held out her arms to her sister only to have Alcida shake her head and back away.

"I did *not* come to you for pity," she said. "In the last six months, Vincent has offered me enough pity to last me several lifetimes."

"You may be misjudging him," Deirdre said, despite her fear that Alcida was right in suspecting Vincent pitied rather than loved her. "The doctor has always impressed me as a kind and gentle man, even though sometimes he appears so overly concerned with his own affairs he becomes oblivious to the feelings of others."

Alcida bridled. "Vincent is not oblivious to others, not in the least."

Deirdre sighed, having forgotten for the moment that while Alcida might feel free to point out Dr. Leicester's faults in some detail, no one else was allowed to do so without risking her anger.

"He probably asks himself," Deirdre said, " 'Is Alcida out?' and his answer must be, 'No, she is not out.' He probably believes every young lady should be given the chance to have her season. Then, too, the fact that you are not out would remind him that you are but seventeen, while he is considerably older. He could believe the difference in ages too great."

"I may be only seventeen, but I'll soon be eighteen." Alcida sighed as she shook her head. "I only wish I knew *what* he thought. Vincent is exceedingly forthright in expressing his opinions on

178

the practice of medicine and on the state of society in general, but he rarely speaks either favorably or unfavorably of other people." Alcida lowered her voice even though they were quite alone in the bed-chamber. "Vincent has told me, however," she said with a satisfied nod, "in an unguarded moment, that he finds Phoebe to be much too full of her-self."

Deirdre paused with her brush raised above her head. "Phoebe does appear to be but little affected by Clive's absence," she said, as she resumed brush-ing her hair.

"I happened to see her do it again today," Alcida said, her voice showing her shock and disapproval. "No more than a quarter hour after mama left the house on her way to make her afternoon visits, Edward called to take Phoebe driving in Hyde Park. That makes at least three times this week. Imagine, three times, and each time when mama was absent. I doubt Mama is aware even now, since she never listens to servants' gossip and I refuse to tattle."

"Do you think your mother would forbid Phoebe to go driving with Edward if she knew?"

"Mama would certainly point out the inadvisabil-ity of spending so much time with one man while engaged to marry another. People *will* talk. And Clive is certain to hear eventually."

"I agree," Deirdre said, "that Phoebe should con-sider the damage to her reputation even if she has no regard for Clive's feelings."

Alcida sighed. "I often wonder if Phoebe behaves as she does, at least in part, because of our father."

"Your father? I have never heard either you or Phoebe speak of him."

"He passed away when I was only four, so I hardly remember him. When I hear his name—Phillip Langdon—I picture a tall, bearded man who smelled of tobacco. Before mother married your father, his portrait was over the fireplace in the library, but now Phoebe has it hanging in her room. Phoebe, of course, was always father's great favorite."

"My mother died of the fever when I was very small," Deirdre said, "so I know how difficult it is to be left with only one parent. Fortunately, I had my grandmother to care for me."

"Our father died of consumption," Alcida said, shaking her head sadly, "when he was only twenty-six. Can you imagine, in a few years Phoebe and I will be as old as he was? Since everyone in the family remarks on how alike he and Phoebe were, I sometimes suspect she wonders if they might be alike not only in manner but in susceptibility to disease as well. She may be afraid she will die young, just as father did."

"What a strange and terrible fear for her to have."

"To my mind, there are no grounds for her fears," Alcida said, "since neither Dr. Taylor, our family physician, nor Vincent has detected any tendency toward a weakness in her lungs." With a shake of her head, Alcida dismissed her own notion. "No," she said, "Phoebe behaves as she does not from fear, but because she enjoys flirtatious adventures, perhaps overmuch. Not only that, but she also pre-

180

fers to have two strings for her bow. While holding Clive in a state of limbo she dangles for Edward, hoping against hope to become mistress of Harmon Hall."

"I suspect the likelihood of her landing Edward is extremely remote," Deirdre said, recalling Edward's expressed lack of enthusiasm for Phoebe . . . if, she warned herself, he had told her the truth.

"Perhaps, perhaps not, one can never be certain of the outcome of affairs of the heart. Edward does seem to be taken with her beauty, at least to some extent. And, of course, since Clive is in Brighton, Phoebe feels at liberty to do as she pleases."

"I was surprised when Clive left town last week to visit his brother, departing so suddenly and with hardly a word of explanation to anyone."

"You must tell absolutely no one this," Alcida said in a whisper, "but his going to Brighton was not entirely his own doing. The visit was recommended and encouraged by Vincent."

Deirdre frowned. "For what possible purpose?"

"To allow Clive a time away from the perturbations of life in London. I suspect something is bothering Clive, perhaps his migraines have returned; but Vincent refuses to give me the slightest hint."

Deirdre bit her lip to stop herself from crying out in alarm. She had never suspected that Clive's trip was anything other than a visit to one of his two older brothers. All along she had thought he was on the path to recovery from the malaise brought on by his lack of memory, a lack making him fear that he had shown cowardice during the Battle of Vittoria.

Leaning down to look over Deirdre's shoulder into the glass above the dressing table, Alcida said anxiously, "Do you notice any difference? Any at all?"

Deirdre considered her sister's image in the glass, wanting to be reassuring, but uncertain what difference Alcida expected her to remark on.

"My face," Alcida said helpfully. "Do you see a change? I applied cucumber lotion three times a day for the last fortnight. Are the scars any less noticeable?"

"There may be some improvement," Deirdre told her uncertainly.

"I think not," Alcida said, turning away from the glass with a discouraged sigh. "How very fortunate you and Phoebe are."

Yes, Deirdre told herself, they were fortunate in many ways, both of them, and both of them were so often selfish, thinking only of themselves. She, at least, should be counting her blessings rather than bemoaning the minor trials and tribulations that came her way in the course of a day. No matter what Clive may or may not have done.

In the same way that Deirdre's thoughts returned again and again to Clive Chadbourne, Alcida's returned to Dr. Leicester. "All Vincent speaks of these days," Alcida said, "is the great good fortune of his inheritance and his forthcoming voyage to the West Indies. If he mentions how overjoyed he is to be leaving England even once more, I shall take this book" — she held up *Pride and Prejudice* — "and hurl it at him."

Deirdre wanted to point out that this was yet another instance of Vincent's lack of sensibility, but managed to hold her tongue. As she went on brushing her hair, her thoughts reverted to Clive. What was troubling him now? If only she could help him!

After Alcida left, proclaiming that she intended to read herself to sleep, Deirdre lay in her fourposter bed listening to the moaning of the December wind under the eaves. As she longed for an end to the protracted sleep of winter and for the reawakening heralded by the coming of spring, her night thoughts returned to a day in her childhood, one of the first warm days in March during her second month in East Sussex.

"Today," her grandmother told her, "we shall walk into the forest to look for wildflowers." She went on to tell Deirdre how she often went into the woods with a trowel and a pail, returning with rich black earth to spread on her garden.

Together they climbed the long hill to the heath and followed the dirt road past the quarry. As they neared the turn just before reaching the bridge over the brook, they heard the thud of hooves and looked up to see a horseman trot around the bend in the road, a horseman who turned out to be not a man at all, but a boy.

"This is Master Chadbourne," her grandmother told Deirdre, when the boy reined in his sorrel gelding.

"Clive Chadbourne of Chadbourne Hall," the boy said, nodding stiffly at Deirdre. How arrogant he is, she thought, and how very handsome.

Her grandmother smiled — she had a lovely smile — and introduced Deirdre. "This is such a delightful day," she said, "we decided to search the forest for wildflowers. Pray join us, Clive."

The boy glanced from the older woman to Deirdre, who hurriedly looked away, then pursed his lips as though to show his disdain for such a feminine activity. Deirdre, expecting him to rein his horse away from them and ride off without a word, was surprised and secretly pleased when he hesitated, shrugged his shoulders, and swung down from the saddle.

Deirdre smiled as she drifted off to sleep, picturing herself walking along the brook at her grandmother's side while intensely aware of Clive a short way behind them, scuffling his feet and kicking small stones so they skittered along the path toward her . . .

*She was on her knees, picking May flowers, small, white fragrant blooms growing on a knoll near the brook. When she had gathered a small bouquet she rose, intending to turn and hand them to Clive.*

*He was nowhere to be seen; she was alone. "Clive," she called, but there was no answer. Where can he be? she asked herself. London. The word sprang into her mind, puzzling her even more. London? Why would Clive be in London when only a moment before he was here with her?*

*Unable to find him, she started to walk along the path beside the brook on her way back to her grandmother's house. A cold gust of wind tugged at her bonnet and she shivered, crossing her arms against the chill. Leaves drifted down around her and she looked up and saw that the trees had* turned from green to an autumn palette of reds, yellows, and golds. The flowers in her hand had inexplicably withered; with a sigh, she knelt to lay them on the ground before walking on.

A lone ash, a tree she had seen many times before, rose in front of her, tall and dark, with only a few leaves fluttering in the wind on its uppermost branches. One of the limbs seemed to point to her right, and so she turned in that direction, following a narrow path that crossed a field, and entered a dark woods.

Ahead of her she saw a small house on the far side of a glade, a deserted woodman's cottage with a gaping black window and holes in the thatch on the roof. She glimpsed a face peering from one of the windows. Was it Clive? The face disappeared before she could be certain. As she started to walk toward the cottage, her long gown tugged at her legs, slowing her, making every step an effort, but she struggled on until she came to the cottage door.

Thinking she heard mocking laughter coming from behind her, she whirled and saw a man lurking in the forest, and recognized Edward, who stood watching her from under the trees, a sword in his hand, an occasional ray of sunlight glinting from the silver blade. He raised the sword, pointing it at her, and she held, afraid. And then he was gone, the woods now seemingly deserted, the only sign of life a large black bird—a buzzard?—slowly circling above the trees.

Shivering apprehensively, she turned to the door, pushed it open, and stepped into the cottage. The single room was empty, the walls rough-hewn

185

wood, the floor under her feet packed dirt. On one side of the room, a fire burned fitfully in a stone fireplace.

"Clive?" she called uncertainly.

There was no answer, but suddenly the fire sprang higher, crackling, the flames curling around the stones and licking up the bare wood walls. How terribly hot it was! Looking around her, choking as she breathed in the roiling smoke, she saw that all the walls were ablaze, fire surrounded her, the flames reaching hungry arms to embrace her.

She turned and ran toward where she thought the door might be, her heart pounding, her breath ragged, ran into the flames. Then the cottage was gone; she stood alone in the cold silence of the night with no notion of where she was or which way she should go.

"Deirdre." A voice called her name from a great distance. She held her breath, keeping completely still, listening.

"Deirdre." The sound was so faint she could barely hear the word, but she recognized Clive's voice. Clive was calling to her; Clive needed her.

Once more she listened, thought she heard Clive call her name again. She ran toward the sound, heard the steady rush of water ahead of her, ran faster, the sound of water louder and louder until it became the roar of a falls . . .


The following afternoon Agnes was helping Deirdre finish packing when Alcida tapped on the open door and came into the bedchamber.

186

"So you decided to go to East Sussex to your grandmother after all," Alcida said.

"To be with her for Christmas." Deirdre hesitated, then said, "Because of a frightening dream I had last night. The actual meaning of the dream eludes me, perhaps it has none at all, but I awoke knowing I must go to—" She paused. "Go to visit my grandmother," she finished after a moment.

Agnes closed the portmanteau, fastened the straps, and stood up. Deirdre thanked her and her maid curtsied and left the room.

"All of us will miss you," Alcida said, "but especially me."

"Alcida," Deirdre said suddenly, "you must spend the holiday with me in the country. Grandmother would enjoy having you."

Alcida brightened, but then shook her head. "Vincent has only a few more weeks before he sets sail for the West Indies. I could never bear to leave him now, when I may never see him again."

Deirdre regarded her with exasperation softened by sympathy. "And what do you expect Vincent to do during these last few weeks of his in England? I believe I already know—he intends to continue to discuss his prospects in the West Indies. Discuss them at great length." She clasped Alcida's hand. "Listen to me, Alcida, you must come with me to the country, if only to give Vincent a foretaste of what it will be like not to have you to talk at or, if you prefer, to talk to."

Alcida frowned and then shook her head. "This will be my last chance to be with him before—" she began.

"He intends to leave you for good and all and you find yourself unable to leave him even for a fortnight? If he cares for you in the slightest, I warrant Vincent will follow you to the country."

"And if he stays in London?"

Deirdre said nothing, letting the meaningful silence stretch on interminably.

"If he stays in London," Alcida said, raising her chin defiantly even as Deirdre thought she detected the glisten of tears in her eyes, "then I will be happy to have discovered the extreme shallowness of his affections. Yes, I shall speak to mother at once; you and I, Deirdre, shall have a delightful time in the country."

# *Chapter Sixteen*

"I look forward to our walk into the forest," Alcida said to Deirdre as they finished breakfast the next morning. "After hearing you talk so often of your rambles in the woods with your grandmother and Clive, I believe I could find my way by myself."

"Be sure you both dress warmly," Deirdre's grandmother advised them. "The north wind is cold today, and these twinges in my arms and legs tell me to expect rain, more than likely followed by snow, before the sun sets."

Bundled in their cloaks and woolen scarves, Deirdre and Alcida set off shortly after noon to climb to the top of the long hill at the edge of the heath.

"I have to be up and doing," Alcida said, "to keep my thoughts from constantly straying to London and to Vincent. What do you suppose he said when he discovered me gone? What will he do, if anything, when my mother tells him I journeyed to the country with you to visit your grandmother?"

Deirdre, forced to wrench her own thoughts from Clive and how she might go about discovering if he was indeed at Chadbourne Hall, as she suspected, belatedly gave her attention to Alcida's problem. "I expect Vincent will ask my father for directions to my grandmother's house," she said after a moment. "He will then delay his departure from London for at least a day or two, not wanting to give the appearance of overeagerness, before coming here for an unannounced visit."

"Do you really think he will? I hope so, I truly do. A day or perhaps two, will he really wait that long before he comes?" Alcida sighed. "I wonder if he will come at all."

Deirdre, feeling a drop of rain strike her forehead, looked up at the threatening sky. "I find that both gentlemen and the weather are impossible to predict," she said, "but at this moment, the weather less so than men. Our best course is to turn back and save the heath and the forest for another day."

"We must at least climb to the top of this hill," Alcida insisted.

The fresh country air must agree with Alcida, Deirdre thought as she watched her sister hurry ahead. She seemed more lively than usual and her cheeks, naturally pale, had a rosy glow.

Alcida, reaching the barren hilltop before Deirdre, twirled around in a great circle with her arms raised above her head. "This is all so lovely," she exclaimed breathlessly, "the heath with its gorse and heather, the hillsides dotted with pines, the copses black and misty, and the stormclouds scudding in the distance with the rain slanting down."

"I agree, the view is quite spectacular. Some even claim, my grandmother, for one, that on a clear and windless day you can see the smoke hovering like a great cloud over London, more than sixty miles away." Hearing the rustle of rain on the dry leaves of the shrubs, Deirdre added, "We must hurry home."

Alcida looked slowly around her, almost, a puzzled Deirdre told herself, as if she never expected to see this vista of hills and heath again and so meant to commit the rural scene to memory. At last Alcida nodded and together they started down the hill. As the cold rain swept over them, Alcida grasped Deirdre's hand and, breathless, they ran hand-in-hand to the house.

"You both must have a hot bath," Deirdre's grandmother told them, shaking her head in dismay at the sight of their drenched clothes. "If not, you may well catch your death of cold."

Later, wrapped in warm robes, they sat in front of the fire in the parlor, sipping hot cocoa. "Probably," Alcida said with a sigh, "this cocoa comes from the West Indies, perhaps from Jamaica, perhaps even from Vincent's own plantation."

Deirdre turned to her grandmother, wanting a change of subject to keep Alcida from dwelling overmuch on Vincent and, more important, eager to discover whether Clive was at the Hall, as her dream had hinted he was. "We should call at Chadbourne Hall during our visit here," she said.

Her grandmother gave her a knowing look before

shaking her head. "It would be all for naught, a wasted trip. The Hall is closed for the winter with only Mr. Albright and his wife, the Chadbourne caretakers, left to look after the house. Lord Moulton always spends the season in town—as you must be aware by now, Deirdre."

"I thought William might have come from Brighton or George from town to spend Christmas in the country." She hesitated. "Or even Clive."

"But Clive is in Brighton," Alcida protested. "Surely you were—" She paused and hurriedly brought a lace handkerchief to her mouth, suppressed a sneeze, and repeated, "Surely you were—" and then did sneeze in a most inelegant manner.

"Chauncey was in the village only yesterday," Deirdre's grandmother said, "and happened to speak to Mr. Albright. The Hall is closed."

Could I be mistaken? Deirdre wondered. After her dream of being in Ashdown Forest with Clive, she had been certain that she would find him here. Perhaps, she told herself hopefully, he was presently at Brighton, but would pay a visit to the Hall on his way back to London. Tomorrow, she promised herself, she would go to the Hall if only the rain, now lashing the windows, stopped by then.

The rain did stop. The weather turned colder in the night, the rain gave way to a snowfall that ended in the early hours of the morning and, when Deirdre wakened, she saw sunshine slanting into her bedchamber. Going to her window, she drew aside the curtain to look out at a world of

192

white, the wet snow clinging to the bare branches of the trees and blanketing the lawn and drive, turning a dark December into an enchanted world.

Alcida did not come downstairs that morning, sending her maid to tell them she had a slight cold in the head and would breakfast in bed. "The cold air and the damp weather," Deirdre's grandmother said, as they climbed the stairs to look in on Alcida. "Unfortunately, colds are often the precursors of much more serious illnesses — fevers, pneumonia, and even consumption."

"A day in bed will cure me," Alcida assured them in a hoarse voice. "I intend to spend my time reading *Pride and Prejudice.*"

Deirdre's grandmother placed her palm on Alcida's brow and frowned. "You shall have a good dose of salts at once," she said in a tone that brooked no protest, "several draughts of warm herb tea during the day and, tonight, a mixture of milk, black pepper, and butter. If that fails to set you on the way to recovery, I have a goodly supply of goose grease saved to rub on your chest."

"I expect to be up and about by tomorrow morning," Alcida told them. "And ready for our walk into the forest on the day after," she said to Deirdre.

"Did she have a fever?" Deirdre asked her grandmother, after they left Alcida's room.

"Only a slight one. My mother always said that sulphur works wonders with fevers and so, if this one persists, I intend to have Alcida drink some sulphur and molasses. You have no cause for concern, Deirdre; your friend should recover quickly."

Later that morning, Deirdre sat beside her sister's bed, reading to her.

"Have you noticed that Vincent resembles Mr. Darcy in a great many ways?" Alcida said. "Although Vincent is much more learned."

Startled, Deirdre quickly raised the book to eye level to conceal her open-mouthed stare. Dr. Leicester? There was no doubt, she decided, that Alcida must be in love, for only one who was love-afflicted could have come to such a strange conclusion. If any gentleman of their acquaintance resembled Mr. Darcy, it was Clive, although fortunately Clive possessed little of Mr. Darcy's overweening pride.

After Alcida nodded off, Deirdre stopped reading and, after a few minutes, when her sister failed to awaken, she leaned over her, kissed her lightly on the forehead, and left the room. Pulling galoshes on over her shoes, snapping and buckling her green barouche coat, tying the ribbons of a fur-lined black Russian-style hat under her chin, and wrapping a green and black tartan scarf about her neck, she left the house, intending to carry out her plan of walking the two miles to Chadbourne Hall. The snow, she had discovered earlier, covered the ground only to a depth of slightly more than an inch.

Following the curve of the entrance drive, she walked past the wayfaring tree at the edge of her grandmother's property and turned right onto a path through a grove of evergreens, the needles from the firs and pines slippery under her feet. After only a few minutes, she stopped as some inner voice seemed to tell her she must go another way; she walked slowly on only to stop once again.

She *must* go into the forest; she knew this in her heart without knowing the reason why. Still she hesitated, but then, deciding, she left the path and walked over the snow between the firs and pines until she came to the clearing at the foot of the hill.

Rather than circling to find the path from the house, she started up the hill, the way steeper here, the coating of wet snow on the slope causing her to slip and slide. The wind swept across the bare hillside, chilling her, but she persevered, following the path to the top of the hill, taking the dirt track past the turn to the stone quarry and into the forest.

Ashdown Forest.

The forest was a vast wilderness of heath, hills, brooks, and bogs; of copses, glens, and glades; of heather, bracken, and gorse; of birch, horse chestnut, ash, oak, and the wayfaring tree; the home of badgers, hedgehogs, foxes, weasels, rabbits, and other small animals. Ashdown Forest was once a part of a much greater forest extending, according to the *Anglo-Saxon Chronicle,* from Kent in the east to Hampshire in the west.

Men had hunted on this land since before history began, the Romans had built roads into this forest to reach the iron mines. The Venerable Bede, more than a thousand years before, had described the forest as "thick and inaccessible; a place of retreat for large herds of deer and swine," the home of wild boars and wolves. Some say the Druids may have worshipped their pagan gods beneath the oaks in the forest; medieval English kings hunted here both before and after King Edward III granted the land to John of Gaunt, Duke of Lancaster.

From the very beginning of her stay in Sussex, Deirdre had loved the Ashdown Forest. After her grandmother showed her the paths and trails near their home, she often ventured into the forest alone. Since she rarely met anyone in this seemingly endless wilderness, she came to consider the forest her own special domain, a magical kingdom peopled by, or so she imagined when she was still very young, fairy tale princes and princesses, Hansel and Gretel, witches, and Red Riding Hood, and as she grew older, by kings and magicians, by knights who, while searching for the Holy Grail, paused to rescue maidens imprisoned in lonely towers.

At first, when Clive, two years after she met him in the forest, began coming year after year to spend his summers at Chadbourne Hall, she considered him an intruder, even though she knew he had been promised the Hall as part of his inheritance and so belonged in Sussex as much as she did. Soon, though, she found herself revealing her secret retreats to him and, later, he led her to his own discovery, the pool below the waterfall in the glen. After that, the forest was no longer exclusively hers; it had become theirs, a place to be shared and marveled over, a sanctuary where they were so often alone together.

Until the day Clive journeyed from London to tell her he was a cavalry officer and that he was betrothed to Phoebe Langdon.

Reliving that terrible moment pained her anew, so she forced the memory from her mind, telling herself Clive was still her friend; she had come to the forest as his friend, and as his sister, if that was how he saw her. At the pantheon — her breath caught as she recalled his kiss — his behavior had not been that of a brother; far from it. Nevertheless, she reminded herself again, the fact remained that he was betrothed to Phoebe.

She paused on the stone bridge over the Miry Ghyll, fondly remembering Clive picking and giving her a wild rose, a rose she still had. She crossed the bridge and, when she reached the other side, saw a single set of footprints in the snow, the recent prints of a man's boots.

Clive, she told herself in triumph, the prints must be Clive's. She should have been surprised, but she was not; nor was she surprised when she followed the tracks and saw them leading away from the road along the brook in the direction of the glen.

After pushing her way through the screen of shrubs, she followed the footprints along the path to the top of the slope above the glen, heard the murmur of water, felt the rapid beat of her heart when she saw Clive far below her. She stopped on the path while still high above the pool to look down at Clive, who was standing on the far side of the Miry Ghyll, gazing pensively into the pool, and saw his image reflected in the pool, his riding boots, his bulky black caped greatcoat, his dark, uncovered hair.

He gave a start when he saw her image in the pool, pausing before he looked up from the water. For a long moment he stared at her as though unable to believe his eyes, then he smiled with the joy of recognition, a smile that made her heart sing. He raised his hand in a salute before striding to the brook, stepping across to her side from stone to stone and climbing to where she waited. As he neared her, his pace slowed.

His smile was gone, his face stern and, Deirdre feared, censorious. She half expected him to ask, "How did you find me?" or demand, "Why are you here?" Instead, he said nothing, reaching out and taking her gloved hands in his as he gazed into her eyes. She allowed him to hold her hands — how could she help herself? — for a long minute before drawing them away.

"I was afraid," he said, "that you might be another figment of my imagination."

When she gave him a questioning look, he said, "I thought I saw Timmons in London last week."

"Timmons?" she repeated, puzzled. Then she remembered and nodded. Lieutenant Timmons was the officer Clive believed he had abandoned to the French at Vittoria.

"It was at night, in that terrible fog. Lieutenant Timmons threatened me with his sword, or at least, it appeared he did, but when I called his name and looked for him, he was nowhere to be found."

Frustration gripped Deirdre, making her shake

198

her head, while in reality she wished she could shake Clive. He should be able to banish these phantoms. Why did he find it so difficult to challenge these demons in his mind, challenge them and slay them? If only she were able to impart some of her strength to him . . .

"Vincent suggested I come here," Clive said, a sweep of his hand indicating he meant Chadbourne Hall as well as the glen and the forest, "and so I did, after visiting my brother in Brighton. Somehow, tramping in the forest seemed different than I remembered it, though—not the same at all." He paused before adding, "Without you, Deirdre."

His eyes met hers and she drew in her breath, expecting him to reach out to her, to touch her. Instead, he looked quickly away, his gaze going beyond her to the snow-covered slope above them, and he said, "We must be on our way. The wind is cold and we may well see another storm before nightfall."

Deirdre, disheartened and uncertain of what to say, remained silent. Clive needs my help, she reminded herself, even though he refuses to acknowledge it. He needs my encouragement even though, if asked, he would probably deny it. More than help or encouragement, he needs me. Yet he refuses to understand or recognize what I can give him. How can he be so blind?

He stepped around her and started up the path, turning to look at her when she failed to follow him. She thought he meant to come back to her, but he merely scowled and said, "Edward bought your portrait." His words sounded like an accusation.

She glanced at him, frowning. Only my portrait, she wanted to say, nothing else. Did Clive believe that Edward's owning the painting compromised her in some way? Surely it did not.

Clive glowered and started up the hill again, and this time she followed him, climbing slowly until she came to where he waited for her at the top. The chill December wind caused her to wrap her scarf around her face to protect her nose and mouth.

"This way," he said, leaving the path and leading her across the virgin snow under the trees to a field where a lone ash stood, one limb seeming to point crookedly to the right.

Deirdre eyed the tree with trepidation. The ash from her dream!

"I came this way once years ago," Clive said. "Were you with me?"

Surely she would remember if she had been, she remembered her times with Clive so well. She shook her head, recalling the tree only from her dream of a cottage consumed by fire.

Veering to the right, he led her into a wood where, after a short walk, she felt a shiver run along her spine when she saw a woodsman's cottage ahead of them on the far side of a glade. Stopping at the verge of the trees, he said, "I found this abandoned cottage while walking alone. I must have mentioned it to you."

Had he? If so, she must have forgotten.

When Clive started across the field toward the

cottage, she glanced apprehensively around her at the encroaching trees, peering into the shadows where, in her dream, Edward had waited, watching her, menacing her.

She saw no one, only the black trunks of the trees outlined starkly against the white of the snow. Relieved as well as annoyed at herself for having such baseless fears, she followed Clive to the cottage. It seemed familiar, but whether from her dream or an earlier, forgotten visit or from Clive describing it to her, she could not tell.

Clive pushed at the warped door and it opened part way before catching. Putting his shoulder to the door, he shoved it all the way open and then stood to one side so she could enter. The inside of the cottage, she saw, was dark. In her mind's eye, Deirdre again pictured flames licking along the walls of the burning cottage, again felt the searing heat of the fire.

Despite her fears, Deirdre drew in a deep breath and walked past him into the darkness.

# Chapter Seventeen

Clive followed Deirdre into the single room of the woodsman's cottage, finding it much as he remembered, with two windows, one in the front and one in the rear, a dirt floor, and a crude stone fireplace. There was a rough-hewn bench lying upside down in one corner; he righted the bench, brushed it off with his gloved hand, and placed it in front of the hearth.

"Wait here until I find kindling to start a fire," he told her, "so we can warm ourselves before walking the rest of the way home."

Deirdre, he noticed, was still looking around the cottage as though she had expected something different, almost as if she had been in this room before and now was puzzled to find it changed from her memory of it. When she gave a start and nodded almost absently, he realized she had only belatedly understood what he had said. Although she glanced down at the bench, she made no move to sit.

Clive walked to the door. He looked back at Deirdre, standing with her arms folded as she stared into the cold grate. How beautiful she was! With a sigh, he forced himself to turn from her and leave the cottage in search of kindling.

Was it possible, he wondered, that Deirdre's reason for coming to the glen had been to search for him? If so, how had she known he was here, rather than in Brighton? Could Vincent have told her? And, even if she knew he was in Sussex, why had she come to him?

The same reason, he told himself, that had brought her with Vincent to the arbor at his lodgings in Bloomsbury. She wanted to offer him her help because it was her nature to help others, but she wanted to help him in particular because she considered him to be almost her kin, a brother in spirit, if not in fact. Perhaps there was another reason—and when he considered this possibility, his heart soared—perhaps she had come because she felt a tenderness toward him that had nothing to do with sisterly affection.

Was it possible, was it really possible? If only it were. But knowing he was betrothed to her stepsister, how could Deirdre have brought herself to defy convention and journey to Ashdown Forest, where they would be alone with one another, far from prying eyes?

Whatever the reason, she had come to him. Thank God.

He had been startled when he had seen her image reflected in the pool in the glen and then overjoyed to discover she was not a figment of his imagination, as Timmons might be, but real, a veritable goddess, just as Joseph Turner had envisioned her, just as Turner had painted her.

I must discover her reason for coming here, he had told himself as he climbed the slope to her. But, reminded of the Turner portrait and having heard the disquieting news that Edward had purchased it, some imp of the perverse—or had it been jealousy?—had instead led him to question her about Edward and she had, quite rightly, lashed back at him in anger.

Chagrined, wanting to delay their moment of parting as long as possible, to give him an opportunity to make amends, he had decided that rather than walking to the bridge and then directly home, he would bring her to this abandoned cottage, remembered from a summer day long ago, to seek brief shelter from the December wind. Noticing Deirdre's distress on seeing the cottage, he had wondered whether she would so much as set foot inside, but although she hesitated in the doorway, she offered no objection.

Clive quickly gathered leaves, twigs, dead brush, and several good-sized logs for the fire, making two trips to bring them into the cottage. Once, while walking along the edge of the glade, he thought he heard a horse whinny in the distance, but although he stopped to listen, the sound did not come again.

He arranged his gatherings on the grate, where the sparks from his flint quickly set the leaves ablaze, and in a few minutes he was able to nod in satisfaction when he saw that the chimney draft was good, so the flames licked up and around the two logs.

Looking over his shoulder at Deirdre, he saw her back away, not from him but from the crackling fire, almost as though afraid of the flames. How unlike her. Did she expect the fire to somehow escape from the fireplace?

"You have nought to fear," he assured her, "the fire cannot spread."

She approached the fire, albeit hesitantly, holding her hands to the warmth. "I had a dream," she admitted, "a foolish dream of danger lurking in the forest, in and around a cottage much like this one. And of fire spreading to destroy the cottage."

"I had my vision of Lieutenant Timmons brandishing his sword," he said, trying to make light of his own unease, "while you have your own unsettling dreams."

"I came here from town to discover whether there was truth to my dream or not."

Had *he* been in her dream? Clive wondered as he nodded. She had not mentioned him, and yet—

"And I intend to return to London later today to seek out Timmons," he told her, "to see if he actually is in town. As I should have done when first I thought I saw him, rather than heeding Vincent."

She sat on the bench, still holding her hands to the fire, while he stood some few feet away, his own hands clasped behind him, his gaze intent on her face. How lovely Deirdre was! Why in the name of heaven had he never really noticed before he'd left Chadbourne Hall to live in London? What a fool he was.

"You came alone," he said, "to East Sussex, to the forest, to the glen." And to me, he wanted to add, but checked himself.

"No, Alcida accompanied me to Grandmama's only to awaken this morning with a cold in the head. So I left her in bed to walk to the glen by myself."

"Alcida came with you?" he asked, taken aback. "With Vincent preparing to leave for the Indies in a matter of weeks?"

"And what precisely did you expect Alcida to do? Stay in London to oversee the packing of his luggage? Accompany Vincent to the dock and dutifully wave goodbye as he sailed away down the Channel?"

He was surprised by her sharpness, her asperity. "Why," he said in some confusion, "I rather expected her to remain at least until Vincent left town. She is quite fond of him, after all."

"I understand the way you think," Deirdre said bitterly. "I understand it only too well because it is so typical of the way men view us. If a young lady happens to show a certain fondness for a gentleman, it behooves her to be at his beck and call at all times, whether it is convenient for her or not, to be available whenever he wishes to have someone to commiserate with him on his failures or to congratulate him on his successes or to constantly remind him how frightfully appealing he is to women, how handsome, how charming, how much of a paragon. To be nothing more than his handmaiden, in other words."

Clive blinked. "Did I say all that? Did I say any of that? Did I even suggest those were my opinions about women and how they should behave? Surely you exaggerate, Deirdre."

"I do not exaggerate in the least."

The tightness of her lips told him she was angry, as angry as he had ever seen her. Why? he asked himself, genuinely befuddled by her attitude. Could her sharpness of tongue possibly be the result of something he had said or done to her? No, surely not. His best course of action was to remain silent, he told himself, even as his perverse imp prodded him into saying, "Then pray, explain yourself."

"Men!" she said, clenching her hands at her sides. "Men think only of themselves, their happiness, their small pleasures of the moment. At the same time, men are blind. They fail to appreciate a tender, loving heart. Alcida is an excellent example. Does Vincent even see her when he looks at her? How can he fail to be aware of the depth of her feeling for him? If not blind, he must be completely heartless."

"Only Vincent is able to speak for Vincent," Clive said. "I cannot. Do you truly expect me to?"

Deirdre looked away from him, but before she did, he thought he detected tears in her eyes. Tears for Alcida? Clive shook his head, once again confused. How baffling women were! Were they unable to state clearly what they meant? Why must they talk in endless circles while never arriving at the nub of the matter?

Even as he sighed in exasperation, he was thinking how lovely Deirdre looked at this moment, so desirable, in fact, that he was quite unable to force his gaze away from her. Was it possible, he asked himself, that she was not referring to Vincent at all, but in some obscure way intended to upbraid him for some real or imagined failing? Even more confused, he crossed his arms over his chest as he resisted an almost overwhelming urge to go to her, to touch her, but realized he must not, nay, could not, so long as he was betrothed to Phoebe.

Clive stepped back from her and from the fire. "The heat," he said in explanation, nodding at the flames.

She seemed to lean toward him only to draw back and slide along the bench away from him. And away from the fire. "So very, very warm," she murmured, loosening her scarf so it draped around her shoulders and then unbuckling the top of her coat. "So warm on one side and yet so cold on the other."

" 'The World Turned Upside Down,' " he said.

She stared at him. "I fail to understand."

"The name of the tune the British military band played at Yorktown when Cornwallis surrendered to the Colonists, to the Americans, was, appropriately, 'The World Turned Upside Down.' Ever since I returned home from the Peninsula, my world has been turned both upside down and inside out. And all because of—"

He paused, wanting to confess to the reason for the change, wanting to say, "Because of you, Deirdre," but Clive, an honorable man, could not bring himself to speak the words.

She caught her breath, almost exactly as he had when first he'd seen her shimmering reflection in the pool at the bottom of the glen. Had Deirdre guessed his meaning without him having to speak the words? She lowered her eyes while he busied himself by using a stick to attempt to revive the dying fire.

If only, eighteen months ago, he could have been granted a glimpse into the future, Clive told himself, how different his life would have been. When he left Chadbourne Hall to spend a year in London, he'd considered Deirdre to be a mere child, an agreeable country companion, a girl with verve and a sense of fun who enjoyed being with him just as he liked being with her, a girl he thought of and treated as the sister he had never had.

In London, he met Phoebe and found himself captivated by her. Everyone, men and women alike, told him that she represented all a man could desire in a woman, for she had beauty, a more than comfortable if not handsome dowry, social position, and, at least when in the company of men, a facile charm and seeming amiability.

When he was her escort, as he often was, he became the cynosure of all eyes. What an attractive couple they made, he heard them say, he tall and dark, she petite and fair. No matter that he realized he might be infatuated with Phoebe rather than truly in love with her—all and sundry assured him it was not uncommon for love to come after marriage rather than before.

Could there, he asked himself, be a young woman in all of London, nay, all of England, more suitable to be his bride? When his answer to his own question was a very confident "No," he spoke to Roger Darrington and then offered for her hand and, to his delight, was accepted. His doubts came later, the first few emerging when he journeyed to Sussex to tell Deirdre his good news, more, some of them well-nigh overwhelming, when he returned, wounded and stricken with self-doubts, to London.

It was then he realized that his world had been turned upside down. He had left England knowing his place among his fellow men, sure of his courage, his valor; he had returned suspecting he might well be a coward who had shamed his uniform while bringing his manliness into question by betraying a fellow officer. He had sailed for Spain with every expectation of marrying Phoebe in the near future; he returned to see her recoil in dismay from the sight of his disfigurement.

Phoebe made him feel he had, in some way, failed her by being wounded and thus scarred when he knew, by God, he had done nothing of the sort. As the days and weeks passed, he slowly came to a dreadful realization: he, Clive Chadbourne, was betrothed to a young lady he did not *like;* he must wed, for he was an honorable man who fulfilled his commitments, someone he could not begin to picture as his companion for the rest of his life.

This revelation was more devastating than if he had discovered a lack of love for his intended bride, since he had to confess to himself that he had never loved Phoebe. In fact, he had never loved any woman except—

Enough. He refused to go on.

Admit the truth, Chadbourne, he told himself— you love Deirdre, you must have *always* loved Deirdre without ever realizing it.

No. Clive shook his head. What he felt for Deirdre was something other than love, unless love was not in the least as he had always imagined it. She had become an obsession with him, she was never absent from his thoughts, he wanted to talk to others about her so he could hear them speak her name, he longed to be with her, to talk to her, to look into her eyes, to touch her, to hold her close and more, much more, all the while knowing he could not, for he was honor-bound to marry

Phoebe.

When he saw Deirdre after an absence, however brief, his heart lurched wildly within him. Her every glance, her every word, had the power to buoy him with hope or cast him down into despondency or fill him with a vibrant sense of anticipation. When he came upon her with Edward at the pantheon in a state of déshabille, he was consumed by anger and jealousy. When he heard Edward had purchased her portrait, he thought she was lost to him forever and he despaired. Were these symptoms of love? He had never dreamed love could possess a man so completely, to the exclusion of all else.

Again he poked at the remains of the logs with a stick, but the fire was almost out; only glowing embers and a few charred bits of wood remained in the grate. He tossed the stick onto the embers and looked at Deirdre, who stood, tying her scarf about her neck while she looked from the window at the darkening forest.

"We should leave while we can still find our way home," she said, turning to face him. "The night comes early in December."

He nodded, watching her, as he did at every opportunity, seeing the last of the light from the fire gleaming in her green eyes, thinking she had never looked more beautiful, with her cheeks flushed from the cold, her eyes aglow, her hair a shining halo around her face.

"We should be on our way," he said, without turning from her, without walking toward the door of the cottage. Nor, he noticed, did she make any move to leave.

"Alcida is ill," Deirdre said. "She must have

awakened by now; I should be at her bedside to nurse her, to read to her.

Clive heard an ember snap in the grate. The only other sound was the thudding of his heart as he gazed, transfixed, into her eyes. What did he see there? Could it possibly be the same message she must read in his? How could he be certain?

He took a step toward her and saw her draw in a quick breath. For an instant he expected her to turn from him, to try to break the spell, to shatter the magic, but instead she hesitantly stepped not back, but toward him.

"I must be on my way to London before dark," he said. Not only to search for Timmons, he added to himself, but to go to Phoebe, however reluctantly.

Deirdre nodded, and his breathing quickened when he saw that her mouth had parted slightly. As he watched, fascinated, she nervously ran her tongue over her lips and he took another step closer to her until only an arm's length separated them. For Clive, her captivating nearness caused the rest of the world to blur and fade away; his world had become Deirdre, only Deirdre.

He started to speak, but he found that his mouth was dry and no words came. He drew in a long, shuddering breath. "Deirdre," he said, whispering her name. And then, louder and more insistent, "Deirdre." And once again, "Deirdre, Deirdre."

She closed her eyes, she seemed to be waiting for him, and he reached for her and took her in his arms, clumsily, awkwardly, for her barouche coat was bulky against his greatcoat. His lips sought hers, his kiss brushed her cheek, her smooth skin

212

warm from the fire; his mouth found her lips, covered her lips, his hand tangling in her hair as he held her to him while he kissed her. And then, to his delighted surprise, her arms came around him as she returned his kiss with a sudden, unexpected passion.

For one long moment there was nothing in the world except the two of them and the wonder between them. Then Deirdre drew back—he gasped from the shock of losing her—and she gave an inarticulate cry, pushed him away, swung away from him, and fled the cottage . . .

She waited for him at the verge of the forest, and when he came to her, his steps slow and tentative, she refused to meet his gaze, turning and walking quickly away beneath the evergreens until she came to a familiar path where they walked side by side in silence, careful to keep a distance, however small, between them, walked past the quarry to the crest of the hill overlooking her grandmother's house, the windows aglow with lamplight.

By the time they reached the front door, they still had neither spoken nor touched. Deirdre put her hand on the latch; only then did she hesitate. He waited. Suddenly the door swung open and they both stared at a flushed-faced Agnes.

"She told me to watch for you," Agnes said to Deirdre in a frightened voice. "Your grandmother did."

Deirdre gasped, and her hand flew to her mouth. "Alcida?" she asked in alarm, grasping Agnes's arm. "Is it Alcida?"

"She's took a turn for the worse, not the better," Agnes said. "The missus sent for the doctor, but only the good Lord knows when he'll come. She's out of her senses, Miss Alcida is. One minute she calls 'Deirdre, Deirdre,' and the next it's, 'Vincent, Vincent.' "

"I shall go to her at once." Deirdre hurried across the entry hall and had started up the curving stairway when she stopped, her hand on the rail, and looked back at Clive, who was still standing in the doorway, watching her. She started to say something to him, but shook her head and turned away, hastening up the stairs, leaving him staring after her. Leaving him behind.

And feeling more alone than he had ever felt in his life.

## Chapter Eighteen

Arriving in London shortly before midnight, Clive idly gazed from his carriage window at the dark facades of the shops along an almost deserted Holborn Street. Not only was he tired to the bone, his mind was in turmoil. He must locate Timmons if the man actually was in London, he told himself, and then he must speak to Phoebe and press her either to name a wedding date or, in all fairness, release him from his obligation.

He looked forward with keen anticipation to finding Timmons, hoping against hope the lieutenant could tell him what had happened at Vittoria. Even if Timmons confirmed his suspicion that he had behaved in a cowardly fashion, at least he would have the satisfaction of knowing the truth.

He looked forward to the meeting with Phoebe, and on the other hand, almost with dread, greatly fearing the outcome would be other than he hoped. Knowing he had acted honorably toward her would provide little recompense for having to spend a lifetime with Phoebe while loving, and not from afar but at rather close quarters, someone else.

His thoughts kept hastening back to Deirdre, to that moment in the abandoned cottage when he'd held her in his arms and kissed her, recalling the unexpected passion with which she had returned his kiss. And then she had fled, shunning him for the remainder of their brief time together. Did she, could she possibly, love him? And what of that bastard Edward? Had she at some time kissed him with the same fervor? Impossible. Or was it?

He smarted when he remembered Deirdre accusing him of being selfish, of thinking only of himself. How untrue! He considered himself the most unselfish of men; she had only to inquire of any of his acquaintances. No one had ever called him selfish before. Compared to most men, he was a paragon of selflessness.

Take Vincent as an example. Though a loyal friend and companion for many years, Vincent did have a tendency to talk rather endlessly of his inherited plantation in the West Indies and the medical experiments he intended to conduct there, allowing his enthusiasms to so narrow his vision that he often gave little heed to poor Alcida. Or to anyone else, for that matter.

Perhaps he should go to Vincent now to inform him of Alcida's illness. No, there was no need, Deirdre or her grandmother would surely send word to Vincent, if not today, then tomorrow; Vincent would learn the disturbing news soon enough; in the meantime, let his sleep, for one night at least, be untroubled. If their roles were reversed, Clive told himself, and Deirdre had, unknown to him, taken ill, he would—

He would want to know at once. Without delay.

Clive tapped on the roof of the carriage with his cane and, when the coachman slid aside the panel, said, "To Dr. Leicester's lodgings in Harley Street, if you please." A few minutes later, he nodded when the carriage turned north from Oxford Street.

Distant churchbells were chiming midnight as he lifted the brass knocker on the door to Vincent's rented rooms. The doctor, on opening the door himself, gave a start of surprise when he saw Clive, but ushered him inside without a word. Clive noted three large trunks in the hall as Vincent led him to the sitting room where an open portmanteau sat in the middle of the carpet.

"You come from Brighton?" Vincent asked, as he poured madeira into two glasses. When Clive shook his head, Vincent said, "From Sussex, then. Did you by any chance have occasion to see Alcida?"

"No, but I bring news of her. And, unfortunately, not good news. I fear Alcida is ill, suffering from a fever."

Vincent, his hand with the glass of wine extended toward Clive, held in place. "Ill? A fever?" His hand shook, causing drops of wine to fall to the carpet. "How is she?" he demanded. "Has she a competent physician? I have reason to realize better than most how lacking in skill many of my compatriots happen to be. Especially those practicing in the country."

"I heard of her illness at second hand; I know nothing more than that she has a fever." Clive hesitated to mention Alcida's delirium for fear of alarming his friend unduly.

Frowning, Vincent stared down at the glass in his hand before setting it aside and nodding to the portmanteau. "I packed this very evening, intending to go

217

to Alcida tomorrow."

Perplexed, Clive said, "Then the news of her illness has already reached you?"

"No, no, I had no notion she was ill." He shook his head. "I must confess, I found myself adrift here in town without her. I wondered, on the other hand, whether her sudden journey to Sussex showed her indifference as far as I was concerned."

"I suspect the opposite to be true."

Vincent brightened. "If so, I have all the more reason to travel to Sussex, now I *must* go to her. I shall depart with the break of day."

"May I offer you a word of advice?" When Vincent nodded, Clive said, "Leave at once, my friend, go without any further delay."

Vincent raised his eyebrows. "Leave at once? Now, after midnight? I shall surely lose my way in that wilderness to the south. Surely the more prudent course is to sleep for a few hours—though God knows whether I can sleep with Alcida ill—and leave at first light."

"Prudence be damned!" Clive gripped his friend's shoulder. "Anyone who contemplates a journey of thousands of miles across the ocean to the West Indies, as you do, can find his way to East Sussex whether by day or in the dark of night. Alcida, I suspect, believes you pity her. If you delay until you receive word of her illness from Sussex and only then leave town, she will, once she recovers, think herself confirmed in those suspicions."

"Pity her? Why should I pity her?" Vincent furrowed his brow in thought.

Exasperated, Clive said nothing.

"Oh, yes, you refer to ravages of the pox. Strange,

but after knowing her for a few weeks, when I looked at Alcida I saw *her* and not her scarred face. She is the most warm-hearted, engaging and, yes, beautiful girl it has ever been my pleasure to meet. Since she is also extremely sensible, she must realize how I feel, even though I may never have told her in so many words." He frowned. "You say she believes I pity her. How very odd."

"True, nevertheless."

Vincent walked to window, looked out into the darkness, and then turned, nodding. "I shall go to Sussex at once. I only pray Alcida will recover from this illness. Certainly I shall do all in my power to make certain she does." Vincent picked up one of the wineglasses and handed the other one to Clive. "To love!" he cried.

"To love," Clive echoed.


On the following morning, Clive appealed to a friend of his father's at the War Office, Colonel Trevor Sturges, for help in ascertaining the whereabouts of Lieutenant Timmons. An hour later he was informed that Lieutenant Warren Timmons had been, until very recently, a prisoner of the French, but had been exchanged for a captured French officer and was now residing at Barnard's Inn.

"You can most always find the lieutenant at the academy at this time of day," Timmons' man informed Clive when he inquired at the Inn. "That fencing academy on Drury Lane."

Driving to Drury Lane, Clive climbed a narrow flight of stairs to an ill-lit hall where a plaque on the wall proclaimed *"L' académie Française d' escrime."*

Opening the door next to the plaque, he found himself gazing into a cavernous room.

He heard the clash of steel against steel, heard fencers in white vests and black masks cry, *"En garde,"* watched them thrust and parry, lunge and retreat. On the walls, crossed swords alternated with portraits of famous fencers and framed certificates awarded to the winners of various fencing competitions.

*"Monsieur?"* A short, moustached man in a blue waistcoat fastened with large gold buttons, looked inquiringly up at Clive. "May I be of service?"

"Is Lieutenant Timmons here?" Clive asked.

"Timmons? Timmons? Ah, yes, but of course." The Frenchman nodded across the room to two men, one obviously an instructor—he was demonstrating a lunging attack—the other his student. Though both were masked, the student had the lean look of Timmons. The two men fenced and, watching, Clive saw that Timmons, if indeed it was he, was proving to be an apt pupil.

Clive crossed the room, heard the instructor say, ". . . to the heart," before both men became aware of his approach. They swung around to face him.

"I say! Captain Chadbourne!" The voice was the voice of Timmons. "Clive Chadbourne."

Timmons yanked off his mask to reveal his thin, long-nosed face and his sandy hair. Holding the mask in his left hand, his glistening sword in his right, he limped slowly, deliberately, toward Clive, who, not knowing what to expect, held his ground, as a tingle of excitement—not fear—coursed through him.

Timmons swung his sword hand to one side, the hand holding the mask to the other, as he advanced.

Clive watched the sword warily, ready to leap from harm's way if Timmons attacked. Timmons, however, did not attack. Instead he flung his arms around Clive, embracing him.

"I say," Timmons said, stepping back and smiling. "I am glad to find you at last."

"Find me?" Clive asked. "I never realized you were looking for me."

"I caught a glimpse of you the other night near White's, or thought I did, in that damned fog, but then I lost sight of you and when I inquired at your home I was told you had taken lodgings in Bloomsbury and when I went there a lady wearing spectacles, a motherly sort, said you were visiting relatives in Brighton."

"When I saw you in the fog, you were brandishing a sword. At least, I thought you were."

Timmons shook his head. "They say London is a dangerous city at night, but surely not dangerous enough to warrant my carrying a sword. What could you have seen?" All at once he smiled. "I say, I have it, in the fog you must have mistaken my cane for a sword."

What a fool I was, Clive told himself. "And then you sought me out?" he asked.

"I never expected to see you again, not alive, not after Vittoria." He glanced at Clive's forehead. "I assumed you were dead; I should have known it would take more than Bony to kill you, Captain."

Clive ran his finger along the length of the scar. "I recall riding toward you, I remember hearing an explosion, nothing more."

"Before you came riding to me to pull onto your horse, I was hit," Timmons said, "once in the arm

221

and once in the leg. I come here to the academy to hone my fencing skills to regain what I lost. Or try to." He smiled. "The Frenchies did this to me; their bloody academy can damn well help me recover."

He led Clive to the window. "Look down there," he said, nodding at the bustling street where clattering carriages hastened past, two horsemen rode side-by-side, urchins scuttled away from a vegetable stand, an organ-grinder strolled past followed by a monkey on a chain—all the ordinary comings and goings of a busy London street at midday. "How marvelous," Timmons said, "and I can enjoy it because of you."

"Because of me?"

"You remember nothing?"

Clive shook his head. "Nothing until I opened my eyes to see a surgeon staring down at me with a rather doleful expression on his face."

"After you went down, one of the French bastards rode at me, his sword raised, shouting bloody murder. You somehow managed to scramble to your feet and shoot him. Then you picked me up, hefted me over your shoulder like I was a sack of meal, and carried me a mile or more toward our lines, looking for help—carried me until you collapsed. I crawled on only to have the damn Frenchies swoop down and take me prisoner. They must have left you for dead, or else they failed to spot you."

Clive gave a sigh of relief, now knowing he had not betrayed Timmons, had not been a coward, had not fled in panic rather than face the enemy. "Thank God," he murmured.

"I should be the one to thank God," Timmons said. "And you, Captain, if there's any justice in this world, should have a medal."

"Hearing your tale," Clive assured him, "is reward enough."

It was just as well that she, her mother, and her stepfather were traveling to Sussex today, Phoebe told herself, for she certainly had no desire to see Edward again after he had acted so abominably in the gazebo. Not that she believed for a minute that Alcida was as dangerously ill as Deirdre seemed to believe, her younger sister *did* have an unfortunate tendency to exaggerate every minor ailment. But with Clive still in Brighton—she expected him to return at any time—and Edward having placed himself beyond the pale with his behavior after he had, in effect, lured her from the party and practically forced her to accompany him to the gazebo, where he had—

No! She would banish Edward from her thoughts and from her life forevermore. His actions had been completely inexcusable. And after she had always considered him to be a true gentleman!

There was a tapping on her chamber door and, when she opened it, Phoebe saw the new maid—JoAnn? Joanna? Annabelle? How could she be expected to remember the name of every last servant?—standing in the hall with a frightened look on her face. The young girl started to speak only to begin stuttering unintelligibly.

Phoebe sighed in exasperation. "Has someone come to visit me?" she asked.

The maid nodded eagerly.

"Clive? Captain Chadbourne?"

Again the maid nodded. "In the—the drawing room," she managed to say.

223

Phoebe flicked her hand in dismissal and the girl hurried away. There was little need, Phoebe decided as she primped in front of the glass, to learn the girl's name since the new maid would most likely be gone before the first of the year . . . if she, Phoebe, had any say in the matter.

When Phoebe entered the drawing room, Clive bowed over her hand and then led her to sit on the couch in front of the fire. How somber he looked! He never seemed to smile anymore, since he was wounded.

She expected him to sit beside her, but instead he chose an overstuffed chair some distance away. A glance at him — she looked quickly away at the sight of that ghastly scar — gave her the impression of a greater self-assurance than he had displayed at any time since his return to England.

"Your mother told me," Clive said, "that you all are leaving within the hour to go to Alcida in Sussex." When she nodded, he went on, "Therefore, I intend to be as succinct as possible." He drew in a deep breath. "We have been betrothed for more than six months, Phoebe," he said, "but whenever I propose setting a date for our wedding, you, for some reason or other, find it unacceptable."

She lowered her head, staring at her folded hands.

"I promised to marry you," he said, when she'd made no reply, "and I fully intend to be faithful to that promise. However, I consider it reasonable to ask you to agree on a date so plans for the ceremony will be able to go forward."

"Unfortunately," Phoebe said, "your illness precludes an early wedding."

Clive rose from his chair. "Not at all." He ran his

224

forefinger along the length of his scar, the wound now white with a faint tinge of pink, as Phoebe quickly glanced away. "As you can see, my wound has healed much faster than anyone, Vincent included, expected."

"That *is* wonderful news," she said, with a decided lack of enthusiasm.

Clive nodded, slowly paced back and forth in front of her. Watching him walk away from her, Phoebe saw his scar reflected in the looking glass between the windows. When he walked in the other direction, she saw the scar in the glass next to the hunting prints.

"More important," Clive said, coming to stand in front of her, "only this morning I solved a troubling mystery when I discovered what happened to me after I was injured, found that I behaved honorably in battle."

Forcing herself to look directly at him, Phoebe bit her lip at the sight of the healed gash on his forehead. Could anyone blame her because her sensitivity happened to be greater than that of others? Phoebe asked herself. She felt tears spring to her eyes.

"I have made a reasonable request, Phoebe," Clive told her, "and I deserve an answer."

Phoebe sprang to her feet and walked to the window where, with tears blurring her vision, she looked unseeing at a carriage waiting on the opposite side of the street. She could never, she realized, bring herself to marry Clive, but in light of Edward's recent unpardonable behavior, if she told Clive the truth, she would be left with no one. She would be alone, all of nineteen years of age and totally without prospects.

She was doomed to be a spinster, she told herself. No, she would be a martyr, much like Mary, Queen of

225

Scots, much like Joan of Arc.

Dabbing at her eyes, she turned to Clive, determined to be brave while realizing what she must do. If only she had a choice!

"Dearest Clive," she said, taking his hand in hers while avoiding looking directly at him, "soon after I accepted your proposal of marriage, I made a heart-rending discovery. I realized my feelings for you were much less fervent than yours for me. In fact, I came to the conclusion I had been unduly swayed by the your earnest and ardent pleas of everlasting love."

"You should have told me," Clive said.

"How, in good conscience, could I?" she asked plaintively. "When you returned from the Peninsula, your health, as you recall, was most precarious, and so I refrained from saying or doing anything that might cause you to sink even further into your slough of despond. Perhaps I was mistaken and behaved in much too tender-hearted a way; probably I should have spoken at once, but I held my tongue to help you in your time of trial and tribulation. If I acted wrongly, dear Clive, I beg your forgiveness. My only excuse is that I did it for you."

Clive gave a small bow of acknowledgment.

"Now," Phoebe said, "with your health fully restored, I must speak candidly and trust that time will heal the wound my words will surely cause you." She looked up into his eyes, endeavoring to avoid seeing the scar. "Dear Clive," she said, "I wish to be released from my vow to marry you. Pray say you will release me, Clive."

He gathered her into his arms and kissed her lightly on the forehead. "Dear Phoebe," he said, "I do release you, I do, I do . . ."

Phoebe watched from the window as Clive left the Darrington house and climbed into his traveling chaise. Had he seemed the tiniest bit relieved? she asked herself. Almost immediately she shook her head. No, of course not, how foolish of her to imagine such a thing. He was a cavalry officer returned from the war; she had mistaken his soldierly ability to conceal pain for relief. How courageously he had accepted what must be the greatest disappointment of his life, she thought, with what a show of bravado. She sighed, but managed to smile wanly, telling herself she had done the right thing. Time would heal the wound she had inflicted.

Moments after Clive drove away, she saw the driver of the carriage that had been waiting on the other side of the street flick his whip. The carriage clattered off, almost as though following Clive's chaise. Phoebe was surprised to see the initials "HH" on the carriage door. Harmon Hall? she wondered. There were no passengers, and though he seemed vaguely familiar, she failed to recognize the driver, a lean young man with a black patch over one eye.

How very strange, she thought, and then immediately forgot the mysterious carriage as she hurried to find her mother to tell her the news of the breaking of her engagement to Clive Chadbourne.

## Chapter Nineteen

Deirdre sat in a straight-backed chair at Alcida's bedside, alternately nodding and opening her eyes only to nod again. Coming completely awake with a start, she rose and leaned over the bed. Alcida was asleep, her face flushed, her skin hot and dry to the touch. To Deirdre, her condition seemed little changed from the night before when a clearly worried Dr. Bledsoe, after prescribing several cups of hot tea and a hot bath followed by a thorough sponging with vinegar, had administered a dose of laudanum and promised to return in the morning.

Deirdre walked to the window and looked out at the stables and the greenhouse and, beyond, the path leading up the hill to the heath and the forest. Thinking of Clive, remembering Clive holding her in his arms and kissing her, warmed Deirdre and then caused her to sigh in hopeless despair. She must put Clive from her mind, she told herself, now and forever.

Hearing an insistent tapping at the door, Deirdre turned in time to see Vincent stride into the room carrying a black satchel. After a glance and a nod at her, he strode to the bed and knelt at Alcida's side, placing his palm on her fevered forehead. Frowning, he took her wrist between his fingers to feel her pulse.

"What did your doctor prescribe?" he asked Deirdre, without taking his gaze from the sleeping Alcida.

After Deirdre told him, Vincent nodded. Unclasping his satchel, he removed and uncapped a green bottle, shaking two large pills into his hand. "Water, please," he said.

Deirdre hurried to the nightstand to pour a glassful from the pitcher.

As she returned with the water, she saw Alcida's eyelids flutter open. Alcida gasped as she stared up at Vincent. "Vincent," she whispered, "I dreamed."

"Here," he said, gently putting the pills into her mouth, "you must take these and then you can tell me about your dream." Holding the glass of water to her lips, he urged her to drink and she did, coughing after she swallowed. "A diaphoretic," Vincent told her, "to induce you to perspire."

"In my dream," Alcida said weakly, "I stood on the shore, my long cape billowing in the wind as I waved goodbye to you until you were lost to sight. I cried. I tried not to cry, but I fear I did."

"Dear Alcida," he said, leaning down and kissing her cheek, "you must forget your dream. I came to be with you and I shall never leave you, never."

"You came because they told you I was ill."

He shook his head. "No, dear Alcida, I discovered life without you was unbearable so I drove all through the night to be at your side." He raised her hand to his lips. "And now," he said, "you must get well. For my sake as well as your own. And I promise you I shall do all in my power to see that you do."

He rose from beside the bed and turned to Deirdre. "I fear the air in this sick chamber has become unhealthy," he told her. "It is a medical fact that the surrounding air must be pure to promote healthy action in the body. A healthy young lady must breathe approximately fifty-seven hogsheads of air every day to maintain the incessant play of affinities between the atmosphere and her organs."

"That is twenty distinct and separate inhalations and exhalations in one minute, twelve hundred in one hour, and twenty-eight thousand, eight hundred each and every twenty-four hours."

"If foul or confined air is breathed instead of pure air, health cannot be maintained and fever often follows. What must be done here is to wrap Alcida well in comforters and quilts and remove her temporarily to another room while this one is well aired by opening the windows and allowing an exchange to take place, pure air for confined air. After a few minutes the windows can be closed, and as soon as the room becomes tolerably warm once more, we shall return Alcida to her bed."

How learned Vincent was! Deirdre told herself as she helped him move Alcida; what good care Alcida would receive from him. When their patient was back in her bed again, Deirdre looked back from the doorway before slipping from the room and saw that Alcida, a blissful smile on her face, had closed her eyes and appeared about to drift off to sleep once more.

The rest of the day passed for Deirdre in a frantic, tiring jumble. Dr. Bledsoe returned and held a long discussion with Vincent in the privacy of the parlor; various friends and neighbors stopped by the house

o offer sympathy and well-meaning advice, usually
suggesting that fevers be starved; and during the
evening, Roger, Sybil and Phoebe arrived, also offering sympathy and similar advice; and servants busied up and down the stairs, some carrying the
luggage of the newly arrived guests while others
brought trays to and from the sick room.

Phoebe, Deirdre noticed, seemed strangely distracted, saying little, but Deirdre was so busy tending
to Alcida that she paid little attention to her stepsister's moodiness. As the house quieted for the night,
Vincent ordered Deirdre to go to bed, announcing
that he intended to sit by Alcida until dawn. Happily,
by this time, his much improved patient was sleeping
peacefully.

When Deirdre entered her own room she found a
small tray containing a cup of hot cocoa on the stand
beside her fourposter bed. Had she asked Agnes to
bring cocoa? No, but perhaps Vincent or even Sybil
had sent the drink to her to calm her and help her
sleep.

After slipping into her white batiste nightgown and
tying the green ribbons at her throat, she sat in bed,
enjoying the feel of the still warm cup of cocoa she
held between her hands. Taking a sip, she grimaced,
preferring a bit more sugar, but she paid the drink
little heed, for her thoughts were on Alcida, overjoyed by what appeared to be her recovery, a recovery,
she was certain, hastened not so much by Vincent's
medicine as by his presence.

She drank more of the cocoa but found it too bitter
to finish. Her eyes began to droop — how very tired
she was — so she placed the half-full cup on the stand,
leaned to one side, and blew out the candle.

231

Settling back on the pillows and pulling the quilt up around her chin, Deirdre sighed as she closed her heavy-lidded eyes, telling herself she should be rejoicing for Alcida's happiness rather than wondering what Clive was doing at this moment, wondering whether his thoughts kept returning to her as hers did to him. So hopeless, she murmured to herself as she slipped into the abyss of sleep, all so very hopeless . . .

She struggled to come awake from a dream of fire, sensing that she was not alone in the room. Was she awake, or still asleep? Was she dreaming, or had an intruder actually entered her bedchamber? She started to cry out, but no sound came. Her vision was strangely blurred, her head abuzz, her thoughts sluggish and confused. She had the peculiar feeling that she was both on the bed and at the same time hovering outside herself, watching and listening, all the while uncertain whether her fleeting impressions were real or merely imaginary . . .

A man strides to her bed, a man who is somehow familiar, stripping the quilt away. She shivers in the chill of the night, she trembles from fear. Attempting to elude him, she discovers herself unable to move . . . a sensation of being wrapped in a blanket . . . strong arms lifting her and carrying her across the room . . .

They descend the back stairs, a single candle throwing grotesque shadows on the walls. They pause in front of a door, the door swings open, snow covers the ground, the December night is cold. Voices whisper, a horse nickers . . . there are two men, one lifting her onto the horse, the other encircling her waist. A low voice urging the horse forward, they ride slowly, at a walk . .

Climbing, the moon a ghostly circle overhead, their pace quickening now to a trot, trees looming darkly in the distance, moonlight silvering the heath, the cold air ever so slowly rousing her from her lethargy . . .

She drew in slow, deep breaths, her mind clearing, realizing suddenly that this was no nightmare. She actually had been abducted and was now a prisoner being carried on horseback in the arms of her captor. Who was he? Deirdre turned to stare into his face.

"Edward," she gasped, fear slithering through her body to gather in a hard coil in her stomach. Her head throbbed and bile rose to her mouth, forcing her to swallow to keep from gagging, dizziness making it impossible for her to twist free of his grasp.

"I mean you no harm, Deirdre," Edward said. "Be patient, we are almost there, and when we arrive, I intend to explain everything."

Her terror waned and mingled with anger. How dare Edward abduct her? She wanted to strike out at him, to hurt him, but her arms and legs felt leaden. She must wait, she cautioned herself, as she tried to think more clearly, her chance to escape would come, it must come; until then, she would let him think she was helpless.

He slowed the horse to a walk again, riding along a dark path between trees and into a forest glade. She stared across the glade in bewilderment. Ahead of them, light shining through a slit at one side of the door, was a cottage, the same woodsman's cottage where she and Clive had sheltered only two days before.

With a shiver, she recalled her dream. "You saw

us," she said without thinking. "You were watching us from under the trees."

"I did follow you," Edward admitted, "you must have seen me."

He swung from the horse, reached up to lift Deirdre down and carrying her in his arms, walked to the cottage and opened the door. Once they were inside she saw, to her surprise, a lamp glowing on a table, several chairs, the bench sitting in a corner, and a fire blazing in the grate. Where had the furniture come from? she wondered.

Edward led her to a chair facing the fire. Once he had seated her, he returned to the door — most likely, she thought, to leave the cottage to tend his horse. Deirdre glanced at the two windows, seeking a way to escape, only to find them boarded over. She looked again at Edward, who stood in the doorway talking to someone outside. Nodding, he closed the door and returned to stand over her.

"I mean you no harm, Deirdre," he assured her for the second time.

She refused to look at him.

"I brought these for you." He knelt to place something near her feet, and when she looked down she saw a pair of slippers on the bare ground. *Her* slippers. After hesitating, she put them on. If she found a chance to escape, bare feet would be a hindrance.

"Would you like tea?" he asked. "I believe it was Sidney Smith who rightly said, 'A man who wants to make his way in life should always carry a boiling kettle.' Tea has been a great civilizing influence on the English." When she made no reply other than to glare at him in a speaking way, he fastened the handle of a kettle on a hook over the fire. She noticed a teapot, two cups, and two saucers on a table near the hearth.

"What I did tonight," he said, "I did for you. At the gallery I promised to make amends for my boorish behavior, and now you witness that atonement."

Not for the first time, she wondered if Edward had taken leave of his senses. Or were his actions the result of a night spent carousing? He did not, however, give any indication of being intoxicated. Perhaps something had happened to him in Canada during his time with the wild Indians. Had he suffered an injury? Or had the loss of a loved one so unsettled him that he had been unable to recover his equilibrium?

He dropped to one knee in front of her, causing her to edge away to avoid his touch. "What greater risk could I take in your behalf," he asked, "than to put my life in jeopardy to ensure your happiness?"

His question startled her, and she stared at him in confusion. He was looking up at her beseechingly, appearing completely sober and certainly not wild-eyed. But she had no notion in what guise insanity might show itself, nor did she know how best to behave when confronted by an insane man — as, she decided, Edward most certainly was.

"From the expression on your face," Edward said, "you undoubtedly believe you are confronted by a man ready for admittance to Bedlam. I assure you, Deirdre, such is not the case. You see before you a man who has never been more sane than he is at this moment."

She shook her head in disbelief, but still said nothing. She would not, she told herself, give way to fear, but instead would harbor her strength and wait for the first opportunity to flee.

"You may not believe me," Edward persisted, "but the idea of bringing you here actually originated with you, Deirdre, although not the rather unconventional manner by which you came."

Now she *was* convinced he must be moonstruck, a victim of lunacy. Although so far he had given no indication of wanting to harm her in any way, she had no assurance this would last. Probably one should try to remain calm in the presence of a lunatic, hoping to soothe him. Would talking to him help?

Edward stood and walked to the fire, where he stared at the kettle. "Will this water never boil?" he asked, more to himself than to Deirdre.

Turning to her, he said, "I recently enjoyed a *tête-à-tête* with Phoebe in our gazebo in town, a rather intimate conversation, I might add, during which she mentioned how you encouraged Alcida to leave town to accompany you in your rather precipitous flight to the country. Since our thoughts, yours and mine, tend to follow similar paths, it became clear to me—"

"They do not follow similar paths," Deirdre said emphatically, her annoyance making her forget her resolution not to upset Edward in any way.

"You, Deirdre, would make Chadbourne a most unsuitable bride—as you will agree if you but give some serious thought to the matter. You and I, on the other hand, are as alike as two peas in a pod."

"We are nothing alike, nothing at all."

"It became clear to me at once," he went on, ignoring her interruption, "the plan you had in mind. You would induce Alcida to leave London and thus force a bereft Dr. Leicester to face the grim prospect of life in the remote isles of the West Indies without her amiable and consoling presence." He looked sharply at her. "I dare you to deny the truth of what I say."

"Something of the sort may have crossed my mind," she admitted.

"Crossed your mind. Ha! You gave the matter considerable thought and planned the scheme in detail before you convinced Alcida, a young and pliable miss, to fall in with your plans."

Momentarily losing her fear of him in the heat of defending her actions, Deirdre snapped, "Her absence did bring Vincent dashing to her bedside."

"Leaving you, Deirdre, I suspect, rather proud of the success of your little stratagem. Deirdre Darrington, matchmaker. Ah, at last," he said, when the kettle began hissing.

Edward used a folded cloth to protect his gloved hand as he gingerly lifted the kettle from its hook. "You must have noted," he said over his shoulder, "how you have influenced me for the better since today I offer you tea rather than champagne. With your help, I might one day become completely reformed." He poured boiling water into the teapot, walked to a corner of the cottage, where he emptied it on the floor, then produced a packet from his pocket and shook tea into the pot. After adding boiling water, he said, "I hope you like Souchong as much as I do."

"I do not want tea," she told him. "Or anything at all from you, sir."

Edward shrugged. "Then, alas, as soon as the tea steeps, I shall have to take mine alone." He clasped his hands behind his back. "I at once realized, of course, that your situation bore many resemblances to Alcida's, with one notable exception: Dr. Leicester had not become betrothed to another while Chadbourne, foolish to a fault, had somehow managed to

237

do so."

Her anger grew. "Clive is far from foolish."

"He is not only foolish, but twice foolish." He poured himself a cup of tea, glanced questioningly at her, and, when she frowned and shook her head, raised the cup to his lips. "Foolish the first time because he asked for Phoebe's hand, twice foolish for not realizing his error and extricating himself from his predicament."

"Clive," she said coldly, "happens to be a gentleman, and gentlemen behave with honor . . . unlike certain others."

"There are many times when the dishonorable. course is preferable to the honorable." Edward sipped his tea, grimaced, and said, "I did forget one thing: the sugar. I do prefer sugar in my tea."

"How long do you intend to keep me here against my will?" Deirdre demanded.

"Not long at all." He drew a watch from his pocket and opened the lid. "The time now is ten past seven," he said. "You should be home by nine, if all goes well." He closed the watch and returned it to his pocket.

"Once I saw how similar your situation was to Alcida's," he said, "I formed my plan to spirit you away from your home just as you enticed Alcida to journey here from London. Recognizing you might not come willingly, I had to resort to rather primitive methods, for which I apologize."

"I would never willingly go anywhere with you!"

"I understand your reluctance, even though it pains me and, more important, is not in your own best interest." He poured tea into the second cup. "In the event you change your mind," he said.

238

"I shall never change my mind where you are concerned. Never."

"I have found that firmness of purpose should be applauded, but plain stubbornness is often evidence of immaturity. At times, Deirdre, you tend to be exceedingly stubborn."

"And you, sir, you are—" She shook her head, so furious that she was unable to conjure up a fitting epithet.

"Let me describe to you what I did," he said. "I sent Cunningham, after disguising him by furnishing him with a patch over one eye, to your friend Chadbourne, to make an offer to reveal a dastardly plot against your person in return for a relatively small sum of money. The bribe was necessary because I find that men value what they are compelled to pay for more than they value what they receive for free. Despite his being somewhat tight-fisted, I expect Chadbourne handed over the money and, with Cunningham serving as his one-eyed guide, is now on his way, post-haste, to this very spot to effect your rescue. He will undoubtedly be armed, and as you can see, I am not, and so, if my timing is even slightly amiss and I tarry here too long chatting with you, he will shoot me down in cold blood. As I said before, I have put my life at risk for you, Deirdre, a fact which you may not appreciate now but I hope will in the future."

She stared at him in open-mouthed astonishment. Did he actually intend her to believe what he was telling her? Evidently he did.

Edward set aside his cup of tea. "In the beginning," he told her, "I decided you would make too many demands on me if you accepted an offer on my part for your hand in marriage. I have, however, changed my mind. Since our time here is short, I must perforce be blunt and eschew the flowery language I would normally use in a situation such as this." He drew in a deep breath. "Will you, Deirdre," he asked, "consent to marry me?"

She stared at him. "Is this another jape?" she demanded.

"Not at all. You would, I have become convinced, make me an admirable wife. If you accept, Deirdre, I offer you in return as much constancy as I am capable of. You might believe my main desire is to see you the mistress of Harmon Hall, but that is not the case. I offer you a life not of tedium, but of travel to the four corners of the globe, a life full to overflowing with surprises and adventure."

She shook her head. "Whatever you offer, I would have to say no, since I love Clive."

"Did I mention love as a requirement? Is there anyone left nowadays who considers love a prerequisite to marriage? Love is overrated, something society uses to describe the veneer disguising passion. Love is of the moment; I offer you a lifetime of devotion."

"I do not want your devotion."

"You *are* stubborn," Edward said sadly. "I can picture you in a few years' time living a life of infinite boredom with Clive, who is, unfortunately for him, a third son. He may well become a remittance man, exiled to some remote corner of the Empire, while you, Deirdre, will be dandling a babe, your fifth in as many years, on your knee."

"I love Clive," she said again.

Edward shrugged. "Which makes him, despite his many shortcomings, a most fortunate gentleman, who should be arriving here within the hour." He took his watch from his pocket and flipped open the lid. "Damnation!" he cried, shaking it. "The watch must have stopped, it still gives the time as ten minutes past seven."

Edward looked up at the sound of a nickering horse. Thrusting the watch into his pocket, he strode to a boarded window and peered through a crack. "It appears I am in for it," he said, "Chadbourne has arrived carrying a pistol and with a most unforgiving look on his face."

# Chapter Twenty

"I had planned to leave you here in the cottage," Edward told Deirdre, "and, to ensure your well-being, remain hidden in the trees until Chadbourne made his appearance. Then I would ride off, leaving the two lovers, the rescuer and the rescued, reunited. Now, if I attempt to leave, I fear Chadbourne will shoot before he asks questions."

"You should have carefully considered the risks," Deirdre said coldly, "before you embarked on such a hare-brained scheme."

Again Edward peered through the slit between the boards. "I see he intends to approach the cottage with caution, as well he should. Perhaps he fears I shall greet him with a fusillade of bullets. I expect I shall have to make a run for it before he comes much closer."

Deirdre, her heart softening toward him—Edward, though misguided, had done this for her, after all, and Clive in his anger might very well shoot him—glanced around the cottage at the single door, the two boarded-up windows, the fire crackling in the grate, and the lamp on the table. She had no wish to have

Edward wounded or killed, but she saw no way for him to leave the cottage except by the only door. And Clive waited for him there.

All at once she remembered her dream of the twisted ash, of Edward watching her from among the trees, of entering the abandoned cottage and then being enveloped in a raging fire. Her dreams, however, did not determine her fate; they were mere signposts toward the future, hints of what might happen as the result of what had already happened. What actually did occur, she realized, depended on her and her alone. She was the master of her fate.

"Is it somehow possible for you to make your escape through the rear window?" she asked.

Edward crossed the cottage to the second window. "Cunningham did his work well, as he always does," he said, testing the boards with his hand, "but the boards are nailed on from the outside. I could climb on a chair and kick them loose, I suppose, but Chadbourne would surely hear the commotion and be waiting for me once I dropped to the ground."

"Clive might not be," she said, "if I set the cottage on fire first."

He raised his eyebrows and then nodded thoughtfully. "Thus making Chadbourne rush inside to save you while I make my escape unnoticed. Ah, Deirdre, a clever plan, one I would have come up with myself after a few more moments. It saddens me to think you prefer to waste your talents on someone not worthy of you."

Throwing off the blanket, she left the chair, blew out the lamp, and sluiced the oil from the lamp's reservoir on the front wall of the cottage. At the same time, Edward hurriedly removed two brands from the

243

fire, using one to set the wall ablaze before holding both aloft until crackling flames started creeping across the bottom of the thatch roof. Placing a chair beneath the rear window, he climbed on it and kicked at the boards with his booted heel. The nails screeched as though in protest. He kicked again and two of the boards swung outward.

Edward put one leg on the sill only to hesitate and draw back. He leaped down from the chair and strode to Deirdre, who was peering through the slit at Clive. Grasping her by the shoulder, Edward spun her around, held her by the arms, and, as she gasped in surprise, kissed her quickly but firmly on the mouth.

Still holding her, he gazed at her for a long moment, shook his head, and then released her to climb onto the chair and clamber through the window. She turned from watching him in time to see the door to the cottage swing inward as Clive burst into the room with a pistol in his hand. The fire crackled around and above her. She felt the heat of the flames and began to cough from the acrid smoke.

Clive paused just inside the doorway to glance around him before striding to her side. "Are you all right?" he asked. When she nodded, he demanded, "Where is he, where is Edward?"

Trying to look dazed and frightened, Deirdre hesitated as long as she dared before nodding toward the shattered window. Clive ran to the gaping opening and blinked as he gazed out into the brightness of sun on snow, raising his pistol only to lower it to his side. Deirdre heard hoofbeats in the distance.

Hurrying to Deirdre's side, Clive thrust the pistol into a pocket of his coat before gathering her into his arms and carrying her from the burning cottage.

Once outside, he strode to the edge of the trees, where he turned and, with Deirdre still in his arms, they looked back at the flames licking along the cottage walls and leaping from the thatch on the roof.

"His life is forfeit," Clive said.

"No!" Deirdre's tone was sharper than she had intended.

"No?" He gazed at her in astonishment. "You defend him after what he did, after what he tried to do?"

"He did me no harm, and I think he truly meant me no harm. I believe he became obsessed. By the painting of Diana, perhaps. I fear that poor Edward, though harmless enough, has taken leave of his senses."

Clive looked down at her with raised eyebrows, saying nothing. Slowly his arms tightened around her and he leaned to her and kissed her, a long, demanding kiss, an exhilarating kiss, wiping away all memory of that strange last kiss of Edward's. She should, Deirdre thought, turn her head away in shocked protest; but, with her heart pounding wildly, she realized she could not, knowing she was where she belonged, in Clive's arms.

He abruptly ended the kiss, leaving her breathless. "Will you," he said, "my darling Deirdre, do me the honor of becoming my wife?"

"But—" she began.

"I saw Timmons in London, discovered him at a fencing academy, of all places, and he assured me that my actions at Vittoria were completely honorable. He even credited me with saving his life. My fears were groundless."

"But—" she said again.

"You need not worry, I fully intend to speak to your father as soon as I return to London, though I feel confident he will offer no objection to our marriage. I rather think he will welcome the news."

"But —" she said once more.

"Phoebe? Ah, Phoebe. I spoke to her only yesterday and you can imagine my happy surprise when she pleaded with me to release her from her vow of marriage. You may be sure I agreed at once, since I long ago realized my mistake."

Deirdre stared up at him, amazed and delighted.

"I love you, Deirdre," he said, "and I always will love you. Only you. I think I must have loved you from the very beginning without having the sense to realize it. I admit I was a fool." He kissed her again, lightly, almost teasingly, the kiss a tender promise. "Will you marry me, Deirdre?" he asked again.

She realized she had failed to give an answer to his proposal, although there had never been the slightest doubt in her mind or in her heart what that answer would be. "Yes," she murmured, "yes, yes, yes."

The warm June sun shone in a blue sky dotted with puffs of white clouds as the bells rang joyously while Deirdre and Clive left the chapel along a walkway covered with white and pink rose petals.

This was not an ending, Deirdre reminded herself, as they drove the short distance to the Darrington house; this was a beginning. All she had ever wished for had come true, she and Clive were bride and groom, she had been joined in holy matrimony with the one man in all the world she loved.

Anything and everything was possible, now that

they would be together for the rest of their lives.

Clive helped her alight from the open carriage and, taking her hand in his, led her through the gate and into the rose garden. The guests from the chapel, she saw, had already begun to gather on the terrace. Her father waved to her and Sybil stopped looking affectionately up at him long enough to smile and nod.

Pausing beneath the arbor, Clive released her hand and reached above his head to pick a red rose.

When he turned to look at her in her puffed-sleeved white wedding gown with its low scooped neckline, the bodice trimmed with pearls, her pearl tiara a brilliant circle of white on her red hair, his breath caught as it so often did at the sight of her. Words inadequately described her; she was the most beautiful, the most desirable woman in the world.

"With this rose," he said, handing her the blossom, "I plight thee my troth."

Smiling, Deirdre held the rose so she could breathe in its sweet, intoxicating scent, her wedding ring sparkling in the sunlight. "Do you remember the last time you gave me a rose?" she asked. "A rose I still have pressed between the pages of a book?"

"How could I ever forget? It was almost a year ago at the bridge in Ashdown Forest on the day we came upon Mr. Turner painting."

Cupping the rose in her hands, Deirdre said, "The same Mr. Turner who at this very moment is making his way toward us with Phoebe on his arm."

The diminutive and rather unfashionably dressed artist bowed to Deirdre, shook hands with Clive, and murmured, in his awkward and rambling way, his congratulations and best wishes. With a shy smile, he looked at Phoebe, whose pale blue satin gown and matching silk bonnet complemented her fair skin and blond curls to perfection. "After much pleading, Miss Darrington has graciously given me her consent," he told them.

"I actually objected most strenuously at first," Phoebe protested, "but Mr. Turner was so charming and persuasive, I had soon depleted my arsenal of arguments."

"Her consent?" With raised eyebrows, Clive looked at Mr. Turner as he echoed his words.

"Why, I agreed to sit for him, of course," Phoebe said, "beginning on Wednesday of next week. For my portrait. Mr. Turner explained that he will insist on exhibiting the finished painting and as a result I may receive considerable unwanted attention; but despite that, I agreed."

Deirdre heard a confused bustling at the doorway leading from the Darrington house to the terrace. As she looked up, she saw two boys carrying what appeared to be a large oblong box emerge from the crush on the terrace and start slowly down the steps. One of the boys saw Deirdre, placed his end of the box on the step and, walking to where she stood, doffed his cap.

"A wedding gift, ma'am," he said, as though repeating memorized words.

"Is there a message with it?" she asked.

The boy shook his head.

"Who sent the gift?" Clive wanted to know.

"A gentleman, sir," the boy mumbled. "He never said his name."

Deirdre walked with Clive to the foot of the steps. The gift, she saw, was some six feet high and three feet wide, but only about six inches deep. Wrapped in white paper, it was decorated with a red ribbon tied in a huge bow.

"What in the world could it be?" Deirdre wondered.

"We shall soon find out."

Clive walked up the steps, undid the bow, and began unpeeling the paper. As he removed the last of the wrapping, he growled angrily and stepped to one side so she could see. Deirdre gasped. The gift was Turner's portrait of her as Diana, goddess of the hunt, depicting her with one hand raised to take an arrow from the quiver on her back while a stag leaped at her side.

Edward had returned her portrait as his wedding gift to her. How unusual! But how like Edward to do the unusual . . . She looked at Clive and, seeing him staring angrily down at the painting, half expected him to smash his fist through the canvas.

"Clive," she said. When he seemed not to hear her, she said his name again. He blinked and walked down the stone steps to her.

Deirdre held the rose out to him. "This rose," she told him, "means more to me than all the paintings in the world. Because you gave it to me."

He glanced at the painting, scowled, and looked at Deirdre, his expression softening. Reaching down, he scooped her into his arms and, skirting the painting, carried her up the steps, across the terrace, and into the house. He strode into the hallway and from there to the deserted music room.

Using his booted foot to shove the door shut behind them, he carried her across the room, lowering her onto a couch and kneeling at her side. He gently cupped her face between his hands.

249

"Our guests," she murmured.

"This happens to be much more important than my guests." He kissed her. As her arms circled him, holding him close, as the kiss lengthened and the world faded away, she had no option but to agree.

It would be gratifying to report that Edward, as a result of being thrown to the earth by a visitation from heaven while on the road to Bath, became chastened and renounced his deceitful and iniquitous ways to become an evangelical Methodist and spent the rest of his life performing good works, much as Saul became the Christian Paul after heavenly intervention while on the road to Damascus. Regretfully, no such miracle occurred and Edward remains unsaved.

He left London immediately after the marriage of Deirdre and Clive in June of 1814, although no one knows whether the marriage in any way precipitated his rather sudden departure.

Since that time he has been reported in Brighton with a young lady on each arm, neither better than she should be; in Paris, France, disguised as a Catholic priest while on a spying mission for the British; in Calcutta, India, where he was supposedly near death as the direct result of leading a dissolute life; in Canada, living once more among the Iroquois Indians; and in the Lake Country, living a hermit-like existence in a secluded cottage while penning his autobiography in iambic pentameter.

Edward may be in one of these places or somewhere else entirely. The only safe prediction that can be ventured is that he is as unrepentant as ever and will probably be heard from again.

Phoebe did sit for Joseph Turner, and her portrait was a great success, although it failed to cause the stir occasioned by the artist's painting of Deirdre as the goddess Diana. As a result of an exhibition of the painting in Queen Anne Street, however, an Irish peer, a handsome, dashing, arrogant gentleman, arranged an introduction to Phoebe, was smitten by her beauty, offered for her hand, and was immediately accepted.

Following the wedding, the couple repaired to the FitzWilliam family estate near Dublin, where they still reside. The Irish, Phoebe discovered, were not as wild and uncouth a race as she had expected. Her marriage, after surmounting early difficulties, including a prolonged visit with her mother during the first year of marriage, has produced one child, a girl named Megan, who gives every promise of being as beautiful — and every evidence of being as spoiled — as her mother.

Alcida did marry Vincent, not in England nor in Jamaica, but on the high seas, the ceremony performed by Captain Hasbrouck of the *Gallant Queen*. After five years in Jamaica, Vincent became convinced that the tropical climate was not conducive to Alcida's good health, so he sold his cocoa plantation at a considerable profit and emigrated with his wife to Philadelphia.

To her deep regret, Alcida, after a series of miscarriages, remains childless. She has, however, become active in Philadelphia society, and is known throughout the state for her charitable work, devoting most of her time to helping orphans.

Soon after his arrival in the United States, Vincent published *Medical Observations and Inquiries into*

*Tropical Fevers,* a two-volume work derived from his experiences in the West Indies. Although the study was based on false assumptions leading to erroneous conclusions, the tomes were received enthusiastically by the medical community of Philadelphia and Vincent soon became one of the most popular and esteemed physicians in the city.

Encouraged and assisted by his wife, he is presently writing *The New Domestic Physician, A Home Book of Good Health,* intended for the enlightenment of laymen. Since the publication of the first of the three projected volumes is eagerly awaited both in Pennsylvania and throughout the other twenty-two American states, a brisk sale is expected and, if the practical medical advice in the book is generally followed, a marked improvement in the health of the populace is anticipated.

Deirdre and Clive, after a wedding trip to Bath, made their home at Chadbourne Hall, where they enjoy visiting and receiving visits from Deirdre's grandmother and from Roger and Sybil Darrington. In the spring of the year after her marriage, Deirdre, much to her and Clive's delight, gave birth to a son, named Clive, followed in the next few years by two daughters. Despite their growing family, they spend the season in London and the summer in Sussex, where they are often seen riding or walking, hand-in-hand, in remote parts of Ashdown Forest.

Clive, after being persuaded by his wife, stood for a seat in the House of Commons as a Whig, was handily elected, and soon became one of the most influential members of that great body. He was instrumental in easing the harsh game laws, limiting the transportation of prisoners for minor offenses and, in later years, reforming the political system by increasing the power of the Commons. It is generally believed that such reform, long promised and long delayed, prevented an armed revolt.

There are those, albeit only an envious few, who claim that the forceful and erudite speeches for which Clive became famous in the House were in fact written for him, in large part, by his wife. The great majority of observers, however, find this unlikely, maintaining that someone as attractive and charming as Deirdre, as faithful and helpful a wife as Deirdre, as caring and attentive a mother as Deirdre, as amiable and gracious a hostess as Deirdre, could not also be as witty and learned as the author of the speeches must perforce be.

When someone, either emboldened by wine or possessed of an abject lack of tact, inquires directly as to the authorship of the speeches, they are met by discreet smiles and a change of subject.

Joseph Turner's painting of Deirdre as Diana, goddess of the hunt, hangs in a place of honor above the fireplace in the library at Chadbourne Hall. The children often observe their father staring up at the portrait with a proud smile on his face.

At other times, however, they see him look at the portrait only to have his face cloud over as he frowns, almost angrily. They have never had the temerity to ask him the reason for his varying responses to the painting, and so to this day it has remained a family mystery.